Phantom
ACADEMY

**ALSO BY
CHRISTINE VIRNIG**

A Bite Above the Rest

Phantom ACADEMY

CHRISTINE VIRNIG

ALADDIN
NEW YORK AMSTERDAM/ANTWERP LONDON
TORONTO SYDNEY/MELBOURNE NEW DELHI

If you purchased this book without a cover, you should be aware that this book is stolen property. It was reported as "unsold and destroyed" to the publisher, and neither the author nor the publisher has received any payment for this "stripped book."

This book is a work of fiction. Any references to historical events, real people, or real places are used fictitiously. Other names, characters, places, and events are products of the author's imagination, and any resemblance to actual events or places or persons, living or dead, is entirely coincidental.

ALADDIN

An imprint of Simon & Schuster Children's Publishing Division
1230 Avenue of the Americas, New York, New York 10020
For more than 100 years, Simon & Schuster has championed authors and the stories they create. By respecting the copyright of an author's intellectual property, you enable Simon & Schuster and the author to continue publishing exceptional books for years to come. We thank you for supporting the author's copyright by purchasing an authorized edition of this book.
No amount of this book may be reproduced or stored in any format, nor may it be uploaded to any website, database, language-learning model, or other repository, retrieval, or artificial intelligence system without express permission. All rights reserved. Inquiries may be directed to Simon & Schuster, 1230 Avenue of the Americas, New York, NY 10020 or permissions@simonandschuster.com.
First Aladdin paperback edition August 2025
Text © 2025 by Christine Virnig
Cover illustration © 2025 by Jay Kim
Also available in an Aladdin hardcover edition.
All rights reserved, including the right of reproduction in whole or in part in any form.
ALADDIN and related logo are registered trademarks of Simon & Schuster, LLC.
For information about special discounts for bulk purchases, please contact Simon & Schuster Special Sales at 1-866-506-1949 or business@simonandschuster.com.
Simon & Schuster strongly believes in freedom of expression and stands against censorship in all its forms. For more information, visit BooksBelong.com.
The Simon & Schuster Speakers Bureau can bring authors to your live event. For more information or to book an event, contact the Simon & Schuster Speakers Bureau at 1-866-248-3049 or visit our website at www.simonspeakers.com.
Cover design by Tiara Iandiorio
Interior design by Mike Rosamilia
The text of this book was set in Adobe Jenson Pro.
Manufactured in the United States of America 0725 BID
2 4 6 8 10 9 7 5 3 1
Library of Congress Cataloging-in-Publication Data
Names: Virnig, Christine, author.
Title: Phantom Academy / Christine Virnig.
Description: New York : Aladdin, 2025. | Audience term: Preteens | Summary: Recently deceased twelve-year-old Finn attends a boarding school for ghosts, but missing home, he and his new friends look for a way out of the Spirit Realm.
Identifiers: LCCN 2024055009 (print) | LCCN 2024055010 (ebook) | ISBN 9781665980364 (hardcover) | ISBN 9781665980357 (paperback) | ISBN 9781665980371 (ebook)
Subjects: CYAC: Ghosts—Fiction. | Boarding schools—Fiction. | Middle schools—Fiction. | Schools—Fiction. | Friendship—Fiction. | LCGFT: Ghost fiction. | Novels.
Classification: LCC PZ7.1.V579 Ph 2025 (print) | LCC PZ7.1.V579 (ebook) | DDC [Fic]—dc23
LC record available at https://lccn.loc.gov/2024055009
LC ebook record available at https://lccn.loc.gov/2024055010

**To my Noodle Friends,
thank you for always
believing in me**

1
Becoming a Ghost

One second, Mom is shouting, "Watch out for the coconut, Finn!"

Next second, I'm dead.

I know I'm dead because the world around me goes *poof*—and disappears. My mom is gone. My little sister, Madison, is gone. Even the evil, coconut-dropping palm tree is gone.

An eerie stillness replaces the cool ocean breeze, and then everything goes black.

Black.

Black.

I can't see a thing!

My ears strain to pick up a sound—*any* sound—but all I hear is the frantic thumping of my heart.

Five seconds pass, then ten, maybe twenty, before the lights flip back on. I blink against the brightness as I take it all in. There is no more white sand. No more ocean. No more mewing seagulls, squealing kids, or sunburnt sunbathers.

In their place two paths now stretch in front of me. Sure as sure, I'm supposed to pick one of them.

Path number one is as wide as a T. rex and is paved with polished teal stones. It heads straight through a field of purple and yellow flowers. Puffy white clouds float in a baby blue sky above it while bright orange butterflies and fuzzy-butted bumblebees dance between the blooms. A huge sign points down this path. It reads: COME THIS WAY! YOU WILL BE REUNITED WITH YOUR GREAT-AUNT EDNA!

The second path, dirt covered and narrow, angles off into a dark forest. A dark forest full of prickly vines and gnarled trees with branches that look like grasping fingers. There are no butterflies or bumblebees this way. Just a murder of crows, *caw, cawing* away.

I spin around, desperately hoping for a third path. A path leading back home.

Back to my mom, who's undoubtedly dissolved into a whimpering puddle of tears by now.

Back to my sister, who's probably wondering why I decided to lie down and take a nap, right in the middle of the beach.

Back to our cramped little house that always smells like Dad's amazing cooking.

Back to my cat and my friends and the neighborhood soccer field and my secondhand PlayStation and my school, Savannah Oaks.

Actually, scratch that last part. Death must be making me nostalgic, because school is one thing I can definitely do without. But I want to go back to the rest of it for sure.

Only there's nothing behind me but a swirling inky blackness. *There is no going back.*

I stomp down my fear, wipe the tears from my cheeks, and face forward again. I need to make a choice.

Of my two options, I know I'm supposed to take the first path—the bright, cheery, flowery one that literally says, "Come this way!" But I remember my Great-Aunt Edna; my parents made us visit her every year on her birthday.

The old lady's breath smelled worse than Madison's diapers, and all she ever wanted to talk about was her cats, each of whom was apparently far smarter and far handsomer than my own cat, Scout.

My dislike for the woman runs deeper than the Dead Sea.

I start down the dirt-covered path, away from Great-Aunt Edna and her vomit-inducing breath.

Away from the too-perfect field with its too-perfect flowers and its too-perfect butterflies.

Toward the terrifying woods that inexplicably feel more welcoming than the alternative.

The moment I step beneath the trees, the temperature drops. Goose bumps erupt all over my arms. My teeth begin to chatter. The trail grows tighter and tighter the farther I walk. Thorny plants reach out and scratch the bare legs sticking out from the bottom of my shorts, leaving deep red gouges.

I know the path is telling me to turn around. To go the other way.

And for a moment, I consider it. Do I have it in me to spend day after day listening to Great-Aunt Edna blab on and on about Snowball? And Mittens? And Mr. Flufferkins?

No. I do not.

I keep walking.

Just when the path gets so narrow I think I'll *have*

to turn around, it opens into a huge clearing covered in grass and thistles and boulders the size of small cars. I take one more step and *zwiiing!* If I didn't know better, I'd think I'd accidentally stuck a fork in an electric outlet. When the shockiness finally wears off, my whole body feels different.

Lighter, maybe?

Flatter?

I'm trying to work out the right word when a *ghost* appears in front of me! I know she's a ghost because not only do the black shoes peeking out from beneath her flared skirt hover an inch above the ground, but her whole body is kinda, sorta, not really see-through.

A high-pitched scream fills the air.

My scream.

Now, normally I'd be embarrassed to shriek a shriek like this, but if ever there was a moment for it, this was it. Because even though everybody knows there is "no such thing as ghosts"—that they're made-up nonsense, same as Bigfoot and Nessie and "exciting" school projects—here I am. Standing in front of one.

Ghost Lady shakes her head. "Just once I'd like to skip the screaming," she murmurs to herself. "Is that too much to ask?"

"But you're a—a ghost!" What did she expect? A fist bump? A thumbs-up? A *How do you do?*

"Look down, Finn."

I'm not sure I should be heeding orders from a ghost, especially a ghost who somehow knows my name, but my eyes dart down anyway.

And another high-pitched screech fills the air. Because *my* sneakers now hover an inch above the ground. And *my* body is now kinda, sorta, not really see-through.

I AM A GHOST!

"Welcome to your afterlife, Finn," Ghost Lady says once my newest round of screams fizzles out. Her voice is stern but not unkind. "I'm Madam Booth. Let's get you settled."

Madam Booth takes off across the clearing while I stand there—or rather, I *float* there—filled with indecision. In their lectures on stranger danger, my parents told me what to do if an unknown adult tried to give me candy. Or if someone in a windowless white van offered to give me a lift home from school. But never, in all their ramblings, did they tell me what to do if I died and a ghost lady wearing a wide-brim hat covered in black feathers asked me to follow her. Talk about a major educational oversight.

In the end, my curiosity (or my impulsiveness, as Mom

would call it) wins out, and I run to catch up. I reach Madam Booth's side just as she crests a small hill. Lying in the valley below is a grand manor with three round, moss-covered towers; a handful of arched windows; and five tall, crooked chimneys that belch out blackish-green smoke. Ivy clings to the mansion like cling wrap.

Madam Booth doesn't pause to admire the view. She heads straight toward the majestic iron gate serving as the only way through the stone wall that encircles the complex like the Great Wall of China.

"What is this place?" I ask as we get closer.

"Your new home."

Madam Booth sticks a tarnished metal key into a rusty lock while I read the words curved across the top of the gate:

PHANTOM ACADEMY
School for Underage Ghosts

2
Phantom Academy

Part of me wants to jump for joy because, really, is there anything cooler than a ghost school? The other part of me wants to kick something—hard!—because what supremely rotten person decided that *even dead kids* need to go to school?

But instead of jumping or kicking, I'm distracted by the millions of questions zipping around inside my head like Legos in a blender. I can't concentrate on anything but getting answers.

"I'm going to live *here*? In a school?"

"Think of it as a boarding school for the dead," Madam

Booth says as she locks the iron gate behind us and starts down the gravel path leading to Phantom Academy's massive front door. "And because you're the fifth new ghost your age to arrive, you and your classmates get to begin your lessons tomorrow."

"Tomorrow?" I groan. In the last thirty minutes I've died, been turned into a ghost, *and* I've been told I need to go to school. Don't I deserve at least one day off to process things?

Madam Booth clicks her tongue impatiently; apparently a groan was the wrong response. "One of your classmates has been waiting almost six months for four more twelve-year-olds from our district to take the path through the woods. So you *are* lucky, even if you don't feel like it."

Lucky? I almost laugh. Nothing about today feels lucky.

Tragic is more like it. Tragic. Or cursed. Or wretched. Although now that the school looms above us, it *would* be rather amazing if we were to get inside by floating straight through the front door.

But nope. Madam Booth turns the handle, and the door creaks open, exposing a vast entry room that looks nothing like any school I've ever been in before.

Instead of crisp white walls, there's dark wood paneling. Instead of easy-to-clean vinyl flooring, there's an ocean of wall-to-wall carpeting the color of a two-day-old bruise.

Instead of obnoxious fluorescent lights, there's a spooky chandelier the size of an elephant, filled not with light bulbs but with candles.

A grandiose staircase, flanked by a couple of hideous vases overflowing with long-since-dead flowers, looms straight ahead. Bookshelves line an entire wall, joined by a handful of velvet-covered chairs and two spindly legged tables. Spiderwebs dangle from the ceiling like the pine-tree-shaped air freshener in my grandma's car. The entire place smells old and forgotten—as though it were a tomb that's been shut off from the world for centuries.

Madam Booth doesn't waste any time as she makes for the stairs, which are covered in a strip of carpeting the color of red wine. "This way, Finn. I will take you to your room."

We float up, up, up until the staircase spills into a long hallway lined with paintings. There are big paintings. Small paintings. Paintings bordered by ornate wooden frames and paintings with no frames at all.

One painting features a dilapidated castle surrounded by a crocodile-filled moat. Another features a serious-looking man with a seriously bushy mustache (a Sir Arthur George Cunningham III, according to the plaque underneath). And a third features an Oscar-the-Grouch-colored dragon sitting atop a mound of gold treas—

Pfffttt.

I hop back, startled. What was that noise? It sounded like it came from *the painting*. I squint closer and gasp. Is that a puff of smoke rising from the dragon's backside?

Did the dragon just . . . fart?

I lean in. And gag. The picture smells like rotten eggs covered in vomit!

Madam Booth clicks her tongue again. Then she continues up a second flight of stairs. Soon we emerge into another corridor brimming with pictures. Madam Booth takes a left, and I follow.

But slowly.

My gaze jumps from painting to painting. There is a man biking up and down a country lane on a unicycle. A horse galloping through a fog-covered field, his hooves *clomp, clomp, clomping* against the ground. A turkey vulture sitting on a dead tree branch, his cold black eyes following me from out of his featherless pink head.

Madam Booth takes several turns before arriving at a dead-end hallway containing nothing but two doors, a candle sconce, a good deal of peeling wallpaper, and a portrait of a woman boasting a mustache almost as bushy as Sir Arthur George Cunningham III's. The woman's dark brown eyes remind me of my mom's, and my shoulders sag.

How long until I'll be able to see Mom again? A few hours? A day? *A week?*

Then I notice how eager Mustache Lady looks. Not only are her dark brown, Mom-like eyes shimmering with excitement, but she's also motioning for me to come closer. I inch toward her picture, and she opens her mouth. "Good day, young sir. I'd love for you to go out—"

"Quit dillydallying, Finn!" Madam Booth is standing in front of one of the two doors, her hands on her hips. "I don't have all day."

I turn back to Mustache Lady, but now that she's noticed Madam Booth, her mouth is clamped shut. "Coming," I moan. I wave goodbye to the painting and go where I'm told. Frankly, it's just like being alive again.

As soon as I'm floating right next to her, Madam Booth knocks on the door,

knock,

knock,

knock,

and opens it, revealing a tidy room with two narrow, wrought iron beds; two antique, wooden desks; a hideous, orange, threadbare rug; and a ghost boy dressed in brown corduroy pants and a maroon T-shirt with READ MORE BOOKS! written across the front in big, block letters. His hair is carefully braided into cornrows.

Ghost Boy looks up from—surprise, surprise—a book. "Hello, Madam Booth," he says politely. Everything about this kid screams teacher's pet.

But then Ghost Boy notices me and his face cracks into a grin so big he looks like one of those smiley-faced emojis. He leaps to his feet, sending his chair toppling backward. The boy whoops and spins in excited circles as his chair clatters to the ground. "We have a fifth! We get to start classes!"

I shoot Madam Booth a questioning look. I'm not too sure about this little roommate arrangement she's come up with. Perhaps I'm not the best match for a kid wearing a READ MORE BOOKS! T-shirt who gets *this* excited about school.

Madam Booth ignores my silent question. "Leroy, this is your new roommate, Finn. Finn, Leroy has been here for a few months already, so he can show you the ropes. You'll get your class schedules at dinner tonight."

As soon as Madam Booth closes the door, I size up Leroy. He might not be my perfect roommate, but that doesn't mean he can't be a good source of information. I look him dead in the eye.

"Okay, Leroy. Tell me *everything* there is to know about being a ghost."

3

The Invisible Whale

"Truthfully? I don't know much," Leroy admits as he sets down his book. I peek at the cover. It's an old Hardy Boys mystery, like the ones my grandpa keeps in his basement next to his antique yo-yo collection.

"You've been here for months, Leroy. You know loads more about being a ghost than I do. Like Madam Booth mentioned dinner. Does that mean we eat? And are these beds merely for looks, or do we sleep? And most importantly, can we go through walls?"

A clever person probably would've waited for Leroy to answer that last question, but instead I take a deep breath, zoom toward the dark green wall closest to me, and *smack!*

As I shake off the violent collision, I realize my poorly thought-out experiment has taught me three things:

1. Ghosts cannot travel through walls. Which is a major letdown, if I'm being honest.
2. Ghosts do not experience pain. At least not the ouch-I-just-smashed-my-nose-into-a-wall kind of pain. Considering the way my gut twisted when I was reminded of my mom's eyes a minute ago, I know *that* kind of pain hasn't gone anywhere.
3. Leroy is actually pretty okay. I must have looked ridiculous bouncing off the wall like a bumper car, but he doesn't laugh. Not one little bit. Instead, he gives me a knowing smile.

"You've tried to run through a wall, too, haven't you?" I ask.

"I have. A wall. A door. A window. Same result as you. Every time."

"Well, that's a huge bummer. But what about the eating and sleeping?"

Leroy hesitates, like he isn't sure how to answer. "We have lights out at ten, and I lie on my bed every night, but I'm not positive that what I do is technically sleeping. And we can eat . . . but it's complicated."

"Okay . . ." I'm trying to stay calm, but it's hard. When I woke up this morning, I thought I was going to spend the day with Mom and Madison, swimming in the ocean and building sandcastles and eating ice cream. Dying and becoming a ghost was decidedly *not* on the agenda. I need to find something good about this new life, something I can look forward to, or frankly, I'm going to lose it.

"What about the pictures in the hallway, then?" I ask. "What can you tell me about them? Like how do they move? And speak?"

"Move? Speak? I have no idea what you're talking about."

I bite my lip to keep from screaming, and that's when I notice Leroy's shoulders. They've started to shake, like he's seconds away from crying.

I reach out awkwardly and give his back a few pats. Which feels *really* weird. It's like I'm touching a water balloon; he's both solid and not solid, all at the same time.

Leroy sniffles a few times before clearing his throat.

"I've been here for three months—*three months*—and I haven't been told anything. Unless it's a designated mealtime or I get special permission to go to the library, it's been all 'stay in your room' every single day. Thankfully, I've got books to distract me from my thoughts, but even so it's been borderline torture. Now that you're here, though, now that there are five of us, maybe things will finally change."

He looks at me like I'm the rainbow at the end of a decades-long thunderstorm.

"Things *will* change," I insist.

I'll make sure of it.

Leroy smiles weakly, but he doesn't say anything else. So I rapidly fill the silence with yet another question: "How long do we have to stay at this ghost school?"

"I asked one of the older kids that same question, and they said we'll be here until we turn seventeen."

Seventeen? I do a little math on my fingers. *That's five more years!*

"They'll let us visit our families, though, right? Like for spring break and field trips and stuff?"

The beads at the ends of Leroy's braids clank softly as he shakes his head. His bottom lip quivers. All at once, I start to feel dizzy. Woozy. Lightheaded. I grab ahold of the closest desk to keep from taking a nosedive.

In five years, Madison will be eight! Will I even recognize her when I finally get out? And will Grandma and Grandpa Winters still be alive? Grandma did have that stroke last year . . .

As Leroy returns his chair to its upright position, I convince myself that he must be mistaken. Madam Booth seemed tough, not cruel. And Leroy himself admitted he hadn't been told anything official. That older kid was probably messing with him. I mean, no school on Earth would keep kids away from their parents *for years*, would they? Even if the kids are ghosts. And even if the school might not technically be on Earth at all, being that I have no idea where I am.

Leroy must sense that I need a moment to decompress because he returns to the world of the Hardy Boys while I collapse onto my bed. I try my best not to think about my family, which obviously means they're all I DO think about.

Madison is probably yelling at my dead body right now, demanding that I wake up and play Barbies with her.

Dad is likely cursing LA traffic as he tries to get to Mom.

And Mom? Knowing her, she's collapsing under a mountain of mom guilt right now, having convinced herself that my death was 100 percent her fault because she'd insisted that we walk to the beach instead of taking the bus, like I'd been begging to do.

I want so badly to let them know that I'm okay—that they don't need to worry—but I can't.

Just like I can't distract myself from my brooding thoughts by exploring the school. Leroy insists we have to stay in our room until dinner, which feels rather a lot like being grounded for doing absolutely nothing wrong.

Perhaps I should have picked the path to Great-Aunt Edna over—

Briiinggg!

I shoot a mile high as a loud ringing sound cuts through the silence.

"That's the dinner bell," Leroy says as he carefully marks his place in *The Clue of the Screeching Owl* with a scrap of paper. He sets the book gently on his desk, and I can't help but wonder what he'd do if he saw the way that I'd haphazardly dog-eared every book I'd ever been forced to read. Have a massive heart attack, probably.

"Let's go. I'll introduce you to everyone," Leroy says as he opens the door.

He takes off for the main staircase, but I quickly veer off into a small alcove, drawn in by a flashy gold frame surrounding a painting of an ocean. The scene looks remarkably like the view I had right before the coconut fell on my head. There is even a palm tree in it. Loaded and ready.

As I watch the waves, an enormous, dark gray *something* comes to the surface. A few seconds later, I realize what that something is: a whale! The Moby Dick exhales and a spout of water shoots from his blowhole. Several droplets of cold mist escape the picture, spraying my face with whale snot.

I laugh and turn to Leroy, whose face is all scrunched up. "Where did that water come from?" he asks.

"From the whale." *Duh!*

"What whale?" Leroy asks, even though *he is staring right at it.*

At first I think Leroy is joking, that he's trying to make me feel silly. But Leroy doesn't *look* like he's joking. He looks like he's seen a ghost.

"You really can't see it? It's right there." I point. "Waving its tail at us."

Leroy shakes his head. "I only see water and sand and palm trees. You really, truly see a whale, though? You're not making it up?"

"Of course I'm not making it up!" I can't quite keep the hurt from my voice. "I'm not a liar."

Leroy holds his hands up defensively. "Okay, okay, I believe you. I've just never heard anyone else talk about these paintings moving. I wonder if you're the only one who can see it."

One thing I know for certain: I can't be the only one. In life I was average at everything. Average at school. Average at video games. Average at soccer. Average, average, average, average. No way I have some unique ability that nobody else has. Maybe only kids with hazel eyes can see the pictures move. Or only kids with freckles. Or maybe Leroy's the only one who *can't* see it. Either way, there's no way it's just me.

I wipe the whale boogers off my face as Leroy tugs at my shirt. "C'mon, Finn. We'd better hurry or we'll be late."

4

My Ghostly Classmates

Leroy leads me to the first-floor dining hall, and I only take one step into the room before my whole body freezes. It isn't the sight of a dark, cavernous room lit only by flickering candles that does me in. Or the reams of Gothic-style wallpaper. Or even the huge mural brimming with creatures that should be relegated to the land of nightmares.

I'm done in by . . . the ghosts! There are *dozens* of them. Floating around the room. Pulling back chairs. Sitting down. *Laughing*.

I should have expected this, of course. But I hadn't.

A whimper escapes my lips as I stumble back. I don't belong here. I should be in my house right now, playing Pro Evolution Soccer on my PlayStation, or eating dinner, or lying on the couch staring at the ceiling.

Clearly someone made a gigantic mistake, because I DO NOT belong in this spooky room surrounded by ghosts!

I feel a hand on my shoulder. My kinda, sorta, not-really-see-through shoulder.

"I know it's a shock, being here for the first time," Leroy says understandingly. "But you'll get used to it soon enough. And you're doing better than most. We get a lot of first-day screamers."

Leroy smiles and motions for me to follow him. As I gulp down my fear and force my legs to move, I can't help but be struck again by how *nice* Leroy is. My friends from school would have laughed themselves hoarse after watching me panic like that.

But not Leroy.

The other ghosts have largely settled into their chairs by now. I spot Madam Booth sitting at the long, rectangular table in the front of the room, just to the right of the entryway. She's joined by about twelve other grown-ups. Some wear clothes like my parents, but many look like they've time machined it here from decades, even centuries, ago.

The remainder of the room is filled with round tables. Five happily chattering kids sit around most of them, but a handful are only occupied by one, two, three, or four ghosts. Despite my still-panicked state, I remember what Madam Booth said earlier about needing five ghosts of the same age for classes to start. I bet these not-quite-full tables are in limbo. Waiting to be filled.

Leroy leads me to a table where three ghosts are sitting, each looking more depressed than the last. One is twisting and untwisting the long, creamy white tablecloth. A second is fiddling with the dead leaves that make up the table's centerpiece. And the third is staring fixedly at her perfectly manicured fingernails. The moment they see me, though, their eyes light up like firecrackers.

"A fifth!" the tablecloth twister cheers. The überskinny boy is sporting too-small Buzz Lightyear pajamas and the worst case of bedhead I've ever seen.

"A fifth!" A girl with leaves and twigs sticking out of her rainbow-colored hair fist pumps the air, the centerpiece long since forgotten. A pair of bright yellow cat-eyed glasses sit at a wonky angle on the tip of her nose.

The third ghost—a girl wearing a fancy dress with an angry black tire track slicing across it—must decide that yelling "A fifth!" would be a bit redundant at this point. She nods instead.

"Everyone, this is Finn. Finn, this is Kevin, Jade, and Rebecca." Leroy points to each ghost in turn.

Before I can even sit, my new classmates start firing questions at me. Chief among them: How did I die?

When I finish my unhappy story, the girl in a fancy dress scoffs. "You died because a *coconut* fell on your head? Talk about embarrassing."

"Like you can talk, Rebecca. Or should I call you Little Miss I-Got-Run-Over-by-a-Scooter-Because-I-Thought-It-Was-a-Good-Idea-to-Take-a-Selfie-in-the-Middle-of-the-Street?"

"Well, at least I didn't fall into a ravine while looking at *a beetle*, Jade."

Jade's eyes widen behind her glasses. "It was a very interesting beetle!"

As Jade launches into a detailed depiction of the insect's markings and how she's 97 percent sure she'd discovered a whole new species, her tablemates' eyes glaze over. Clearly this is not the first time they've heard this tale.

"I died when my dad's pet rattlesnake got out of

its cage," Kevin whispers to me, even though Jade is still talking. "And Leroy here has no idea what did him in."

"Really?" I ask Leroy. "You have no idea at all?"

"None. One minute, I was reading a book while sitting next to my parents at my brother's baseball game. And the next minute, I was dead."

"And before you ask," Jade chimes in, apparently finished with her beetle tirade, "he wasn't eating anything, so he couldn't have choked. Leroy doesn't remember drinking anything, so it was unlikely to be poison. My theory: a foul ball did him in."

Before I can wade into the mystery of Leroy's death, Madam Booth appears at our table. "Your schedules for tomorrow," she says as she drops five identical pieces of paper onto our table. My new classmates attack them like piranhas.

Once the dust settles, I grab the remaining sheet and look down.

Grade 7 Daily Schedule

8:00 a.m.: Breakfast
9:00 a.m.: Reading ~ Room 11 with Madam Booth
10:00 a.m.: Writing ~ Room 11 with Madam Booth
11:00 a.m.: History ~ Room 11 with Mister Gruber

PHANTOM ACADEMY

12:00 p.m.: Lunch
1:00 p.m.: Be the Best Ghost You Can Be ~ Room 11 with Madam Lecter
2:00 p.m.: Haunting 101 ~ Room B8 with Mister Zilla
3:00 p.m.: Intro to Electives ~ Room 11 with Mister Morte
4:00 p.m.: Free time
5:00 p.m.: Dinner

"Writing? Reading? History?" I grumble. "How boring."

"Agreed," says Jade, who is practically bouncing in her chair. "If we have to have 'normal' subjects, why can't they at least be biology or entomology or science? Haunting 101 sounds amazing, though, doesn't it?"

Leroy winces at the word "haunting," but before he can say anything, a *ring-a-ling* draws everyone's attention to the staff table. Madam Booth stands there with a tiny silver bell in her hand. Everyone quiets immediately.

"The only announcement tonight is that we have a new student, Finn Winters, seated over at Table Eight. He is the fifth new twelve-year-old, so Table Eight will begin classes tomorrow."

A slew of envious looks fly in our direction. Shoot, am I the only one at Phantom Academy who isn't obsessed with school?

"Now eat!" Madam Booth instructs.

When I was alive, I would have happily stuffed my face 24/7 if my parents had let me. But now? I'm not the least bit hungry. And I become even *less* hungry when a red-haired ghost in acid washed jeans and an oversized, button-down shirt floats by and plops a pile of brown mush on my plate. The stuff smells like rancid fish sautéed in dog poop, and it looks even worse than it smells.

"What is this?" I ask.

"Dinner." Rebecca rolls her eyes.

"Yes, I know it's dinner. But what *is* it?"

"I call it brown mash," Kevin says happily as he shoves a forkful into his mouth. "But I have no clue what it actually is."

I can't peel my eyes away from Kevin's pale white throat as he swallows his first bite. Because he is kinda, sorta, not really see-through like the rest of us, I can watch the mash slide down his neck until it disappears beneath his Buzz Lightyear pajamas. My brain can't help but imagine the mash continuing its journey to the very, very end. Which brings up an extremely important question.

"Hey, do ghosts poop?"

Rebecca gags. Jade laughs.

"We aren't technically alive," Jade says as she absentmindedly pushes up on the bridge of her glasses. Not that it helps; when her hand falls away, the glasses are every bit as wonky as they were before. "So we don't *need* to eat at all. I suspect we only have mealtimes because they give us something to do. And because some people, like Kevin over there, would miss eating too much otherwise. But to answer your question, yes. If you eat, it needs to come out eventually."

"And in case you're wondering," Kevin says through another mouthful, "our bodies don't actually *do* anything to the food. Everything looks *exactly* the same coming out as it did going in."

Rebecca gags again. "You guys are so immature!" She looks over at the table next to us where three girls are giggling as they ogle a boy on the far side of the room. It doesn't take an Einstein to figure out that Rebecca desperately wishes to join their table.

"Ignore her," Jade whispers to me. "She hates the rest of us almost as much as she hates beetles. Now try the mash. I'm not going to pretend it's as good as my abuela's empanadas or anything, but it does taste slightly better than it looks."

5

Pink Dress Girl Points the Way

By the time I leave breakfast the next morning with the rest of Table Eight, I've learned several things about being a ghost:

1. Ghosts do not need to shower. Or brush their teeth. Or wash their faces. High fives all around, right?
2. Ghosts do not change their clothes. *Ever!* All I can say to this is zip-a-dee-doo-dah am I ever glad I was wearing shorts and a T-shirt when that coconut fell. There's this kid who sits on

the far side of the cafeteria who must have died on Halloween. He gets to spend the rest of eternity dressed as a giant red lobster!
3. Pooping as a ghost is weird. *Really* weird! I'm not sure I ever want to do it again.
4. I now understand why Leroy wasn't sure if ghosts sleep. I don't know if what I did last night was sleeping either.
5. Ghosts cannot cry. While lying in bed last night—trying to sleep, or to not sleep, or to do whatever it was I was supposed to be doing— it hit me (or smacked me, more like it) that I was dead. That I'd never get to talk to my family or friends again. That I'd never be old enough for Mom to let me head a soccer ball. That there would never be a present for Finn Winters under a Christmas tree again. But despite my heart feeling like it was being torn to shreds by a great white shark, not a single tear fell.

And now it's morning and my feet are dragging—not literally, of course, being that they're an inch above the ground—as I follow my classmates through the halls of

Phantom Academy. Heading to a reading class, of all things.

After several minutes of left turns and right turns and more left turns, Leroy skids to a stop. "Wait a second. Does anyone *actually* know where Room 11 is?"

The four of them look at each other.

"I was following Rebecca," Kevin says.

"I thought you were leading." Rebecca gestures toward Leroy.

"I was trying to follow Jade," Leroy admits.

"And I'm just happy to finally be out of my room," Jade says, shrugging, "without having to sneak out, that is."

As the four of them start arguing, movement in the painting behind Leroy's back catches my eye. A blond-haired, rosy-cheeked girl dressed in a ruffly, pink dress smiles as she points to her left. She looks uncannily like Rebecca. *If* Rebecca knew how to smile.

Sidestepping my quarrelsome companions, I tiptoe over to Pink Dress Girl. "Are you saying Room 11 is that way?" I ask, indicating the direction she'd pointed.

Pink Dress Girl nods, nearly sending her wide-brimmed hat—which is covered in pink and white roses—toppling off her head.

"Thanks," I whisper as I turn back to my classmates. "Hey, people. I mean ghosts. We need to go that way."

Rebecca snorts. "You've been here less than a day. How would you know?"

I gesture toward the painting. "She told me."

Silence fills the hallway.

"Umm . . . *who* told you?" Jade finally asks, even though Pink Dress Girl is now waggling her eyebrows and puffing out her cheeks.

Cripes, could Leroy be right? Am I really the only one who can see the pictures move?

Pink Dress Girl makes a monkey noise while scratching her armpits, and still, nobody reacts.

How can they not see it?

Or hear it?

I study my classmates' faces. None of them have hazel eyes or freckles, so . . .

Jade is still waiting for me to answer her question, but thankfully, Leroy jumps to my aid. "It's not like the rest of us have a clue where to go. We might as well follow Finn."

"*Or* we can return to the dining hall and ask for directions." Rebecca spins around and takes off down the hallway, Kevin following in her wake like a puppy. Jade stands there uncertainly for a minute, then does a funny little hop-jump thing as she turns around. And trails after Kevin.

"Okay, you're up," Leroy says as he motions for me to take the lead.

I head down the hallway in the direction Pink Dress Girl had indicated, but soon we come to a T in the road. Leroy looks anxiously behind him, no doubt trying to decide whether he still has time to catch up with the others, but I'm not giving up that easily. Not with a painting of a farmer hanging right in front of me.

I clear my throat. "Sir, do you know where Room 11 is?"

The man ignores me completely as he works to corral a dozen clucking chickens into their pen.

"Hey, farmer man? With the chickens? Can you help me?"

Finally, the man's eyes look my way. "Are you talking to me?"

"Of course. I need help finding Room 11. Can you give me directions?"

The man's eyebrows knit together, like he can't quite believe what he's hearing. In his distracted state, three chickens sneak around him, heads bobbing up and down with every step.

"Oh shucks," the farmer grumbles. "There go Gladys, Gertrude, and Rose again."

Leroy starts wringing his hands. This is taking way too long.

"Room 11?" I ask for the third time, and finally the farmer comprehends my question. He tells me to turn right, and that my destination will be halfway down the hall.

"Thank you." I smile.

"Why are you thanking a wall?" asks a voice that most definitely does not belong to Leroy.

I spin around and find a girl approaching. She's got to be no older than ten, and based on her expression, you'd think she caught me picking my nose or putting on a tinfoil hat or burping the ABCs.

Obviously, I can't tell her the truth. She'd totally crack up.

"Why was I thanking a wall, you ask? Well . . ." I rack my brain for an explanation that doesn't sound totally absurd. "The wall holds up the school, right? Don't you think it deserves our thanks?"

I'm not sure who cringes harder, Leroy or the farmer. Even the chickens stop bawking so they can revel in my humiliation.

The girl doesn't even respond. She simply gives me one more strange look before turning around. And floating away.

"Now *that* was entertaining." Leroy's voice shakes in amusement. "I think you were smart not to tell her you were talking to a painting, but you could have said you were thanking *me*. Not the wall."

"Thinking on the spot has never been my strong suit," I admit. "But at least I got the directions. We're almost there!"

A minute later, Leroy and I arrive at Room 11, a first-floor classroom that looks like it belongs in a history book. The desks are tiny and cramped. The only lighting is a couple of tall, narrow windows and some oil lanterns. And instead of a SMART board or a whiteboard, it's a chalkboard that sits in front of the room.

Madam Booth is the only other ghost there.

Leroy and I slide into the old-school desks—which somehow make sitting on a pile of thumbtacks seem comfy—and watch the door. My brain automatically expects to see my friends from Savannah Oaks parade into the room, and a hollow feeling settles in my chest when I remember it's not them who I'm waiting for, but Rebecca, Kevin, and Jade. Five minutes later, mere seconds after the bell rings, the three of them finally shuffle into the room.

Jade grins when she sees us. Rebecca sticks her nose in the air.

"I expect you all to be on time from now on," Madam

Booth says sternly as my classmates settle into seats. "Now, let's start class."

I raise my hand.

"Yes, Finn?"

"Why do ghosts need to take a reading class? I mean... we're ghosts."

Jade murmurs "Exactly!" under her breath, while Leroy looks at me like I'd just declared peanut M&M's to be disgusting.

"Do you know what 'bellicose' means, Finn?"

I shake my head.

"'Evanescent'?"

I shake my head.

"'Interpolate'?"

I shake my head.

"You could be a ghost for one hundred years, two hundred years, or even longer if you so choose. Reading is a great way for ghosts to pass some of that time, and it helps to have a good vocabulary and a critical reading mind."

"Isn't that why dictionaries were invented?" Jade murmurs so only I can hear. The two of us, at least, seem to be on the same page.

"And before you ask about writing next hour, it's the same with that. Many ghosts are prolific writers. In fact,

I suspect several of your favorite authors are dead. Like Michael Nickelback, a Phantom Academy graduate."

Leroy gasps and almost falls out of his chair. "Michael Nickelback is dead?" he squeaks. "And he went to school here?" He looks down, clearly wondering if Michael Nickelback's ghostly butt once sat upon the same chair he is sitting in now.

As Madam Booth rattles off a bunch of other famous authors who wrote their masterpieces as ghosts, Jade turns to me. "Do you know who Michael Nickelback is?"

"Not a clue."

Madam Booth clicks her tongue at us, and then she's off. Teaching.

Learning about reading and writing in ghost school turns out to be every bit as mind-numbingly dull as Language Arts class is in normal school, so I pass the time doing more interesting things.

Like seeing how long a ghost can hold their breath. Answer: indefinitely.

Trying (and failing) to feel my heartbeat in my wrist.

And plunking my kinda, sorta, not-really-see-through hand smack dab on top of the page I'm supposed to be reading and attempting to make out the letters through all my bones and sinew.

(Sinew. How's *that* for a first-rate vocabulary, Madam Booth?)

When the bell finally *briiingggs* at 11:00 a.m., Leroy is the only one who looks disappointed.

Our next ghost teacher glides into the room, and I almost burst out laughing. Mister Gruber is wearing khaki pants, a red and orange argyle sweater, purple socks covered in dog faces, and flip-flops. It's like he died while trying to decide whether he wanted to go to the beach, a circus, or a chess game at the park.

Once Madam Booth leaves the room, Mister Gruber claps his hands three times—*clap, clap, clap*—and smiles a smile that looks every bit as real as the abominable snowman.

"Settle down, class," he says, despite the room already being dead silent. "I'm here to teach history. Over the next several years, you'll learn about ancient civilizations, about decades-long ghost wars, about the rise and fall of kings. But first, we'll cover something a little closer to home. During these next few days, you'll learn the history of Phantom Academy itself."

Even though I'm in school, and this is *history* class (aka Snoozeville), I find myself leaning forward. Unlike reading or writing, the history of Phantom Academy is something

CHRISTINE VIRNIG

I *want* to learn about. Maybe Mister Gruber will confirm how long we'll all be stuck in this school. Maybe he'll talk about all the visits home that Leroy didn't know about. And maybe, just maybe, he'll mention the moving paintings!

6

Sir Arthur George Cunningham III

Mister Gruber launches into a lecture about how Phantom Academy opened its doors in the 1700s. How it was the two hundred twenty-second ghost school to open its doors. How there are now ghost schools servicing every region of the world, including one for Antarctica!

He tells us that each ghost school is a little different. Some focus on children, some focus on adults, and some take everyone. In the case of Phantom Academy, it takes kids five through seventeen, which confirms the first part of what that older kid told Leroy.

I raise my hand.

"Yes, little ghostling," Mister Gruber says.

Little ghostling? Really?

"What happens to kids younger than five?" Madison is only three; if an evil palm tree decides to do her in tomorrow, where will she end up? In a day care called Little Boos, perhaps?

"Under-fives do not get the option to take the trail through the woods. They all go the other way."

"Where does the other way lead?" Jade asks.

We all hold our breaths, dying to know what we passed up when we chose our path. Apart from an eternity of listening to Great-Aunt Edna babble on endlessly about her fur babies, what would my life—er, death—have been like right now? Would I still be sitting in a classroom? Or would I be scarfing down heaping plates of nachos and gigantic bags of pink cotton candy while chilling out between rounds of the most colossal game of laser tag ever witnessed by mankind?

"Next time, raise your hand," Mister Gruber tells Jade in a firm voice. "And we do not know where the other way leads."

"Nobody does?" Jade asks in surprise. Mister Gruber gives her *a look*, and Jade's hand shoots up in the air. When

Mister Gruber finally nods in her direction, she repeats the question.

"Only those who take that path know where it leads. And they do not come back to report upon their findings."

As this news sinks in, Mister Gruber starts talking about Sir Arthur George Cunningham III. Mister Gruber says Sir Arthur is the most important person in Phantom Academy's history, which explains why his picture sits at the top of the main staircase.

I raise my hand, but Mister Gruber keeps talking, going on about how Sir Arthur was a rich baronet who traveled across the Atlantic Ocean in the early 1700s. How he loved the British Empire and was King George I's staunchest supporter.

I begin waving my arm around like it's a windshield wiper, but Mister Gruber continues to ignore me. He explains how Sir Arthur died in 1721 from an infected paper cut. How he founded Phantom Academy a decade later. How he was headmaster for one hundred ninety-nine years, at which point he moved on.

I stick my left hand in the air next to my right, like I'm on a roller coaster, poised to barrel down a massive drop. This two-armed strategy finally works, and Mister Gruber looks my way. "Good heavens, this class is inquisitive," he says in a way that leaves no doubt as to whether he means this as a compliment. (He does not.) "Go ahead. Ask your question."

"Is Sir Arthur related to Mustache Lady?"

"Mustache Lady?" Rebecca snickers under her breath.

Mister Gruber sighs. "I'm going to need you to elaborate."

"You know, Mustache Lady. There is a portrait of her on the third floor near Leroy's and my room. She's got a mustache that looks almost as big as Sir Arthur's."

Mister Gruber frowns. "Sir Arthur did have a sister with a mustache, yes. Josephine Cunningham, her name was. She was a school cofounder, but we do not talk about her."

Five hands shoot up. Nothing makes a subject more interesting, after all, than knowing it's off-limits.

"We do not talk about her!" Mister Gruber repeats. And one by one our hands drop back to our desks.

For the rest of class, my head spins with thoughts of Josephine. Why won't Mister Gruber talk about her? And why did her brother get all the credit if they *cofounded* the school? Was her mustache not bushy enough?

Eventually, the bell rings and we're off to lunch. The same red-haired ghost I saw last night at dinner is plunking a yellowish-brown, rectangular thing onto everyone's plate. For an instant, he looks in my direction and my eyebrows shoot up. He's hardly any older than I am!

"Why doesn't he go to class?" I ask Leroy as I jerk my head toward the boy.

"You mean the cook? He graduated decades ago."

Leroy's words stop me dead in my tracks. I hadn't thought about it before, but if ghosts don't change their clothes, that must mean they stop growing. Stop changing. So even after I've been a ghost for ten, twenty, a million years, I'll still look like the same pale, freckly faced twelve-year-old I am today. I can't decide whether this is good news... or bad.

I plop into my usual seat at Table Eight and immediately plug my nose. Today's lunch smells like a pile of festering hot garbage! Oh, how I miss my dad's mac and cheese.

And his homemade pizzas.

And his deluxe grilled cheese sandwiches.

And his chocolate chip cookies, which were *to die for*. I'd happily put up with ghost pooping every day for the rest of my death if those ooey-gooey circles of goodness were on the menu.

I smile as I think of Dad in the kitchen, all decked out in his bright red STAND BACK, DAD IS COOKING! apron.

And then I promptly *stop* smiling as I realize that if Phantom Academy has its way, it could be five years before I get to see him like that again. FIVE YEARS!

As my mood sours with the injustice of it all, my festering-hot-garbage lunch is no longer the stinkiest thing in the room. I simultaneously want to cry, and scream, and throw my yellowish-brown rectangle across the room and watch it break apart against the mural of nightmares.

"You okay, Finn?" Jade asks, distracting me from my thoughts. "You look like you're feeling some real feels over there."

"It's just, don't you all miss your families? Your old lives?"

Kevin gulps down the last bite of his lunch and grins as I slide my untouched plate in front of him. "I don't know. When I was alive, my parents pretty much ignored me all the time. They were too preoccupied with my jock of an older brother and my perfect little sister. Sometimes I wonder if they've even noticed I've died yet. Really, I think I prefer being dead."

"I, for one, miss my old life a lot," Rebecca says. "I miss Manicure Mondays and Shopping Saturdays. I miss updating my *thousands* of BuzzHive followers every day. Oh, and Daddy promised to buy me a black Bugatti when I turned sixteen. I was really looking forward to that."

"*And* you miss your family, right?" Jade asks.

Rebecca shrugs. "My parents were never home. It's hard to miss someone you never saw in the first place."

My eyes sting as I think about Kevin and Rebecca being ignored by their parents. That must have been terrible. Maybe I should give Rebecca another chance before I completely write her off as a stuck-up, self-centered snob.

"Oh, but I do miss this game that Daddy and I played when he was in town and actually wanted to spend time with me," Rebecca says excitedly. "We'd go downtown and make up nicknames for the homeless people sleeping in the park. Like Bag Lady Betty and Shoeless Shaun. That was fun."

And there was Rebecca's second chance, officially blown.

As Kevin dives back into his lunch and Rebecca resumes her favorite pastime of ignoring the rest of us, Leroy, Jade, and I discuss our families.

Jade's house had apparently been teeming with people—her five siblings, her grandma, her parents—but she misses her papá most of all. His one and only fault, per Jade, was his rather wishy-washy opinion of beetles.

Leroy also lived with his grandma, along with a brother and his parents. "My nana would totally blow a gasket if she could see what qualified as food here," Leroy reminisces as he side-eyes his plate. "She can be really scary, too, if she wants to be. If she were here, she'd have them serving us fried chicken by dinnertime."

"That would be nice." Fried chicken doesn't sound nearly as good as Dad's chocolate chip cookies, but it would still be an improvement. "But don't you two think it's rotten that we can't visit our families?"

"Yeah, being dead has been way better than I thought it would be—apart from these stupid things—" Jade pushes up on the bridge of her cat-eyed glasses. As usual, they don't move at all. "They must have slid down my nose when I fell into the crevasse, and now they're stuck in the most irritating position. It's like dying with a giant wedgie and being helpless to fix it."

I cringe at the thought. Wedgies are the worst!

"But being dead would be so much better if we could check out of this place from time to time," Jade continues. "I know the teachers get to leave campus because I've overheard them talking about seeing their grandkids and great-grandkids and great-great-grandkids and stuff, so there has to be a way to get home."

I perk up immediately. "We need to find it!"

Even as Jade sits up straighter, Leroy seems unsure. "I

don't know." He fiddles with one of his braids. "We can't be the first kids to miss their families. Don't you think others have tried to leave before? I bet this place is locked up tighter than Alcatraz."

Jade's head tilts to the side. "Didn't three people escape from Alcatraz, though?"

Leroy frowns. "Well, yeah, *technically* I suppose they did. But according to this documentary I watched, a lot of experts think they drowned before they reached the mainland. So they probably aren't the best role models."

"It's not like we can get any more dead than we already are," I argue as Jade nods along, clearly just as on board with escaping as I am. "Say what you want, Leroy, but I'm getting back home. No matter what."

I've never been more serious about anything in my life either. Because even though I agree with Jade that being dead isn't that bad—I mean, there are no scary, scythe-wielding Grim Reapers roaming the hallways; no three-headed dogs guarding the front door; and no half-hippo, half-lion Devourers of the Dead lurking in the bathroom—the fact remains that I'm essentially being imprisoned *in a school*.

And . . . I miss my mommy.

Suddenly I'm almost as excited as I am sad. I have a

quest, just like a character from one of Leroy's novels. And sure, I might not be that into reading, but I still like *hearing* about adventures as much as the next kid. And now I have one of my very own!

Feeling too giddy to sit, I push back my chair. According to the creepy, spiderweb-encrusted grandfather clock in the corner of the room, there are twenty minutes left before I need to be back in Room 11. "I'll meet you all in class. I'm going to drop this off in my room quick." I hold up my history book, which must weigh almost as much as a pregnant rhino.

The first time I pass Mustache Lady's portrait on the way into my room, she's sleeping. A soft snoring sound oozes out from her canvas. But when I come out of my room five minutes later, Josephine Cunningham waves me over.

I'm at her side in a jiffy. "Yes?"

Mustache Lady's Mom-like eyes twinkle as she bows slightly. Her curly brown hair is piled high atop her head, and she's wearing a dress that looks like a cross between a silk nightgown and a potato sack. "Good day again, young sir. If I might be so bold, I wish you to go out—"

Josephine's mouth slams shut faster than a Venus flytrap.

"Go where?" I beg, but her eyes have lost their sparkle. And they're no longer focused on me. They're looking at something *behind* me.

I twirl around.

And gasp.

A ghost—dressed head to toe in black—stands motionless in the main hallway, staring at me and Josephine. And his expression? Let's just say it doesn't make me think of a kindly grandfather or fun uncle. It's all corners and edges. Like he's channeling his inner Darth Sidious.

"Are you conversing with that portrait?" His deep, rumbling voice is as soothing as a hurricane.

I don't need to be told that this is *not* a ghost I should open up to. "What? Conversing with a portrait? Of course not, sir. That would be ridiculous. I was, umm, well, I was talking to myself. Yeah. I was staring at the wall, talking to myself. I do that sometimes when I'm bored."

Kind of like how I babble when I'm nervous, apparently. For someone with the "impulsiveness of a house cat," as my mom liked to say, I really should get better at talking myself out of jams.

Not surprisingly, Scary Ghost Dude doesn't look convinced by my rambling nonsense. He *tap, tap, taps* a finger against his chin while studying my face. I try to look innocent, but I'm pretty sure I look more like I'd just accidently ripped a big one.

"Josephine Cunningham, huh? What an interesting painting for you to be standing in front of."

"Josephine who? I'm only here because that's my room." I point at my closed door.

"You're this close to your bedroom, and yet you chose to talk to yourself in the hallway? That is no less interesting."

I have no clue how to respond to that without making an even bigger fool of myself, so I carefully maneuver into the main hallway and back away from him instead. Slowly at first, then faster and faster and faster. When I reach the main stairs, Scary Ghost Dude still hasn't moved. He's laser-eyeing poor Mustache Lady like she stole his lightsaber.

Except wait a second . . . he's not *completely* still, is he? His lips are moving!

Which means *he's* now conversing with Josephine. Either that or he's decided to give the whole staring-at-a-wall-and-talking-to-oneself thing a try himself. I strain my ears and pick up a few phrases. Phrases like "It can't be" and "Wasn't that disproven?"

I don't hear any hint of Josephine's voice, so I'm pretty sure we're solidly in talking-to-oneself territory. I'm trying to decide if I can risk floating back toward Darth Sidious to better listen in when his gaze shifts from Mustache Lady to me, causing my stomach to coil like a string of bright red wrapping ribbon.

Decision made, I shudder and race down the stairs. All while wondering *what* can't be. And what, exactly, was disproven.

7

The Rules of Ghosthood

"Whoa! You look freaked out," Leroy says as I slide into the desk next to him in Be the Best Ghost You Can Be class (or BTBGYCB class as I decide to call it from now on; it rolls off the tongue better).

I shove my still-shaking hands into my pockets. If I close my eyes, all I see are Josephine's lips as they sealed up tighter than a bank vault when Scary Ghost Dude came up behind us.

"I *am* freaked out." I start filling Leroy in on what happened in the hallway.

"No way! You were talking to *a painting?*" asks Jade, who apparently has better hearing than an elephant. She gets up from her seat several desks over and moves next to me. "Was it a painting that gave you directions this morning too?"

After the day I've had, I'm not sure if I should be snitching on my own ability or not. But if Jade and I are going to be Prison Escape Buddies, I probably shouldn't be keeping secrets from her. I nod.

"That's amazing! But I think you were smart not to tell that ghost what you can do. I'll bet—"

The classroom falls silent as the door opens and a ghost wearing a light blue hospital gown glides into the room. Even for a ghost, she's super, duper pale. As she turns around to drop a book on her desk, I'm beyond relieved to see that her gown is fully tied shut in the back. My one and only other experience with a hospital gown was when my grandma had her stroke; and let's just say that gown showed waaay more of her backside than I ever wanted to see.

"She died the day after her only child was born," Jade whispers. "Sad, huh?"

"Very," I agree. I can still remember how over-the-moon happy my mom was right after Madison was born. Going from *that* to *dead*, all in one day? "Sad" doesn't do it justice.

The teacher turns back around and grins cheerfully as she introduces herself as Madam Lecter. Unlike seemingly every other adult in the building, Madam Lecter appears genuinely happy to see us.

My shoulders relax. My hands stop trembling.

I like her immediately.

"Be the Best Ghost You Can Be probably sounds like a terrible bore of a class," Madam Lecter says, and I can't help but agree. I'm expecting her to make us sit in a circle and talk about kindness. And about our feelings. And about how important it is to get along with one's fellow ghosts. A bunch of gag-me-with-a-spoon type stuff.

"But actually," Madam Lecter continues, "in this class you'll learn about all the things you can do after graduation. You have so many options, so many ways you can pass your time. I think you'll find the possibilities invigorating! But before we get to all that, first I've been tasked with teaching you the all-important rules of ghosthood, which we will review every single term until you can recite them in your sleep."

For all of two seconds, I'm shocked. *Ghosts have rules?* But then I remember that nothing about becoming a ghost has been what I expected. There are schools. Teachers. We have to *read* and learn history. I haven't been allowed to see my parents. *Of course* there would be rules.

PHANTOM ACADEMY

Madam Lecter flips over the chalkboard to expose a black surface already covered from top to bottom in an elegant script.

THE THREE RULES OF GHOSTHOOD

1. Ghosts must never, under any circumstance, harm the Living.
2. Ghosts must never, under any circumstance, materialize while in the presence of the Living.
3. Ghosts must endeavor, at all times, to keep their existence hidden from the Living.
   a. If the Living sense a ghost and use simple means to get rid of them (asking them to leave, smudging with sage, etc.), the ghost should strongly consider leaving; if they opt to stay, they must be extra careful to avoid detection.
   b. If the Living call in a priest, shaman, or other paranormal expert to do a banishing, a ghost MUST leave the space. There are no exceptions.

*FAILURE TO FOLLOW THESE RULES CAN RESULT IN A GHOST BEING FORCED TO MOVE ON!

Hands fly into the air.

"Yes, Rebecca?" Madam Lecter says.

"Mister Gruber mentioned something about moving on too. What does it mean?"

"Great question!" Madam Lecter says. Rebecca beams like she's a genius, even though her question was the most obvious question in the history of obvious questions. "Moving on is like the ghostly equivalent of death. It ends your existence as we know it, and you move on to whatever comes next . . . *if* anything comes next. Most ghosts eventually grow tired of their time here and move on voluntarily, but if you break the rules? You have no choice."

A shiver races down my spine. Ghosts can *die*? A quick glance around the room confirms I'm not the only one shaken by this revelation.

But Madam Lecter merely gives us a knowing smile. "Don't worry about moving on right now, okay, class? Most of you will choose to remain a ghost for dozens or even hundreds of years, and you'll learn all the details about moving on later in your education. Do you have questions about anything else though?"

Why yes. Yes, we do. Once we recover from the shocking news of our continued mortality, we start grilling

Madam Lecter. Unlike Mister Gruber, though, she loves our curiosity.

We learn that "the Living" is the proper way to refer to not-yet-dead people.

We learn that ghosts can share space with the Living, but we must try to keep our presence hidden. If we don't, the ghost government will come after us.

We learn that there are several reasons why the Living might suspect a ghost is around. These include:

- Seeing a ghost. Madam Lecter says there is a special way that ghosts can become visible to the Living, but doing so violates the second rule of ghosthood and "no honorable ghost would ever do it."
- Photographs. If we aren't quick enough at getting out of the way of a camera, we can show up as a smudge.
- The temperature. If we get too close, the Living can sometimes detect the icy coldness that radiates off us. (For the record, I call boloney on this one. My temperature feels perfectly normal, thank you very much!)
- Moving or misplaced items. As oblivious as the

Living tend to be, even they will notice if a book moves across the room right in front of their face. So we ghosts should never use an object while the Living are around. But if we accidentally put something back in the wrong spot after we're finished with it? Madam Lecter says this is usually fine. The Living tend to blame misplaced items on their awful memories. Or on their kids. Or on the dog. (Madam Lecter says that some ghosts make a sport out of hiding people's keys and wallets and phones and socks, but that this is cruel and we *should not do it*.)

- Animals. Cats and dogs can often sense when a ghost is nearby, and occasionally, the Living will pick up on their pets' behavior. Usually, though, they simply think their animals are "acting weird."
- Loud noises. If we drop a book or bang pots and pans together, the Living will hear it. If we yell super loud, the Living will hear it. If we talk normally, though, we'll be fine. (Unless we've gone and done what no honorable ghost would ever do and we've made ourselves visible to them; then the Living can hear us as clear as day.)

"Yes, Finn?" Madam Lecter smiles. "You have another question?"

"I do. I've heard we aren't allowed to leave Phantom Academy until after we graduate, but if that's true, why are you teaching us how to interact with the Living now?"

I cross my fingers under my desk, hoping Madam Lecter will say I've clearly been misinformed because obviously we'll be leaving campus all the time. Instead, she blathers on about how these rules are the most important thing we'll learn during our time at Phantom Academy, so despite them not being personally relevant quite yet, the headmaster—whoever that is—believes students should be taught them early and often.

I slump in my chair, but my classmates don't let up as they keep firing question after question. "Our housekeeper once thought there was a ghost living in her bathroom," Rebecca says, "so she smudged our entire house with sage. Did that do anything to the ghost?"

"Not a thing," Madam Lecter answers happily. "Nothing the Living does affects us in any meaningful way. But they *think* their actions—whether it's smudging or ringing bells or burning our prized possessions—impact us because we take these acts as indicators that we need to be more careful."

"I've heard that ghosts are stuck near where their bones

are," Kevin says dubiously. "So if a priest is called in, how can we leave the area?"

Madam Lecter shakes her head. "The Living have such silly notions about the dead. We are not connected to our bones, or any other object for that matter. Otherwise, how would you all be here? No, as long as you follow the rules, you're only limited by your own imagination."

Slowly her words sink in, and I stop fiddling with the orange thread hanging off my shorts. Does this mean that once I figure out how to break out of Phantom Academy, I can go anywhere I want? Of course I'll go home first to spend time surrounded by all my favorite things—like my family; my cat; my stuffed giraffe, Raffi—but after that?

Can I visit the top of the Eiffel Tower? Haunt the end zone at SoFi Stadium? Ride X2 over and over again at Six Flags Magic Mountain without waiting in line?

For the first time all day, my classmates and I are nothing but smiles.

But then the door opens again and in slides Scary Ghost Dude in his head-to-toe black. As his gaze settles on me, the smile falls right off my face.

"I'm Mister Zilla," he declares. "I'm here to take you to your next class."

8
Room B8

We get in line behind Mister Zilla and follow him down one flight of stairs. Then a second flight of stairs. He takes a left and we glide along a long, twisting corridor that's far darker and far narrower than any I've seen upstairs. Instead of pictures decorating the walls, there is nothing but endless stone and the occasional candle bracketed to the wall. The air is cold and smells like damp, moldy earth.

Eventually, Mister Zilla stops and gestures toward a doorway.

The doorframe itself looks like any other doorframe

in the school, but what's *inside* the frame does not. Instead of a door, it's a shiny, shimmering *something* that fills the rectangular space. It looks like the surface of a soap bubble.

"I must grab something from my office," Mister Zilla says. "Go on through, all of you, and I'll be along shortly."

He walks away, leaving the five of us gaping after him.

Leroy takes a step back. "Do you think it's safe to walk through that? I don't think it looks safe to walk through."

"Stop being a chicken," Rebecca huffs. "Mister Zilla said to go through, so it must be safe. He's a *teacher*."

Rebecca walks up to the doorway, acting all brave, but she doesn't step through. She goes right back to staring at it.

"Who's the chicken now?" I ask. As my classmates shrink back, I slowly extend my hand toward the shimmering barrier. No way I'm waiting until Mister Zilla returns to investigate.

"Are you sure you should do that?" Leroy asks as I inch my hand forward. My fingers, my palm, my wrist, disappear. I yank my arm back, relieved to find all five fingers still intact.

Figuring there's no point in putting things off any longer, I take a deep breath (even though I don't *need* to breathe) and mummy walk through the barrier. The faintest of shocks shoots through my body as I pass to the far side, but I have no time to dwell on the sensation because I have a whole new problem to worry about: My arms—which I can *feel* sticking out in front of me—have vanished!

I look down. The rest of me is gone too!

As my invisible fingers start trembling, I realize they aren't *actually* invisible. I can still see the faintest of outlines. It's just that instead of being kinda, sorta, not really see-through, I'm now kinda, sorta, *almost completely* see-through.

I start breathing easier, and then Rebecca enters the room. Being that she's as near-invisible as I am, I might not have noticed her at all . . . had she stayed quiet.

Which she most definitely does not.

"Finn? Finn?" Her voice rises in panic. "Finn? Where are you?"

"I'm right here, Rebecca." I jump up and down in front of her. Rebecca's eyes narrow for a second before growing to the size of apple fritters. Then she glances down. And shrieks.

And her shrieks, by the way, are *much* more solid than the rest of her. They bounce off the walls and worm their way into my brain.

I'm about to stick a finger in each ear when a terrified

voice calls from the other side of the door. It's Jade, asking Rebecca if she's okay. It's a very valid question, considering Rebecca still sounds like she's got her hand stuck in a garbage disposal, but Rebecca is way too busy screaming to respond.

"We're fine," I yell over the noise. "You can come through."

Jade, Kevin, and Leroy pour through the shimmering barrier, and the expected several minutes of chaos ensue. Finally, though, everyone calms down.

"I can see you better now than before," Jade observes as she squints at me.

"Hmmm. I see you better too." My classmates are still super translucent, but they're much easier to make out than they were when we first arrived in the room. It reminds me of the way a person's eyes adjust to the dark.

"What an odd classroom," Kevin says. And he's right. There are no desks, no pencil sharpeners, no chalkboards. Instead, the room is full of couches, chairs, and a bookshelf overflowing with books. There is a kitchen area with a stove and a sink. A messily made bed and a dresser. A table with a glass bowl filled with plastic bananas sitting on top of it. A window with long, flowing curtains that somehow looks out upon a walled-in courtyard, even though I'm pretty sure we're in the basement's basement.

Even stranger than the furniture is *how* everything looks. With the exception of us ghosts, the whole place is brighter. It's as though someone turned up the lights. Or added a couple extra layers of paint.

I start walking over to touch a banana—which is Madison's most favorite food in the entire world—when Mister Zilla floats through the door. For a second, he looks as near-invisible as the rest of us, but then he scrunches up his face and *poof*. He looks exactly like he did back in the hallway!

"Whoa, how did you do that?" I ask.

Mister Zilla gives me a cold glare, so I quickly raise my hand. Which Mister Zilla ignores.

"Everyone, go stand by a chair or couch," Mister Zilla orders.

We all scurry to do what Scary Ghost Dude says. I pick a comfortable-looking red chair and float awkwardly beside it.

"Now . . . sit!"

I try to do as I'm told, but things don't work out so well. As soon as my butt hits the fabric, it goes right through! I'm falling, falling, falling until *splat*. I look around and am relieved to find I'm not the only one lying spreadeagle on the ground. Or an inch above the ground, to be exact.

Mister Zilla sits on a hard-backed chair (*his* butt does not fall through!), and a smile spreads across his face as he watches us scramble to our feet. Unlike Madam Lecter's kind smile, his looks more like Scar's from *The Lion King*.

Mister Zilla waits until we're all looking at him before spreading his arms wide. "Welcome, class, to the Land of the Living."

9

The Land of the Living

The Land of the Living? It sounds like the name of a video game. Or an old TV show. Or some dreadful fantasy novel.

From my classmates' expressions, I'm not the only one who's never heard of this place before.

Mister Zilla must notice our confusion because he promptly elaborates. "The Land of the Living is where most of you will live once you graduate from Phantom Academy."

"We're going to live in Room B8?" Kevin blurts out.

Mister Zilla looks at the ceiling, and I'm pretty sure

he's making himself count to ten before responding to Kevin's question.

"No," he says finally. "You will not live in a classroom. Room B8 is simply a tiny pocket within the Land of the Living, which is the place where all of you resided before you died. It's what you might call 'the real world.' Room B8 is meant to show you what things will be like once you're back there again, this time as a ghost. Now stop asking questions and look around."

He doesn't need to tell us twice. Leroy walks over to the sink and tries to turn on the water. His hand goes straight through the handle. Jade jumps onto the bed. And winds up on the floor. I grab a book from the bookshelf—which, come to think of it, is more of a Leroy thing to do—and come up with a handful of air.

"Why do we need to bother with reading class if we can't even pick up a book?" I mumble to Jade. Like, really. That's just mean.

Mister Zilla drifts over to us. "In this class you will *learn* how to pick up a book. And turn on a tap. And lie in a bed. Although I doubt any of you have the concentration needed to master these skills any time soon. I suspect it will take a while." He huffs, like we're already a grave disappointment.

With every word out of my teacher's mouth, I hate him more. I can concentrate fine, mister!

"Wait a minute," Jade says. "If this is the Land of the Living, where is the rest of the school?"

I stop my silent ranting to pay attention. It's a good question. Where *were* we before?

"The rest of Phantom Academy exists entirely within the Spirit Realm. Had you died many thousands of years ago, you would have spent most of your ghosthood there. But thanks to the Thirty-Second Ghost War, most ghosts now live entirely among the Living. The Spirit Realm is reserved for things like schools and government offices and a handful of highly exclusive ghost resorts."

Mister Zilla's words make me wonder . . . How many ghosts are floating around in the Land of the Living right now? Before I died, was I sharing my bedroom with a ghost? Did I walk past a handful every day on my way to school and not know it? Were any ghosts watching that time I ran up to a woman in the grocery store and hugged her leg, thinking she was my mom, only to discover she was a total stranger?

Before I can ask, Leroy speaks up. "If this is part of the Land of the Living, what if a human walks in right now?" He looks around the room like he's expecting his favorite not-yet-dead author to walk through the front door at any second.

"This is a protected space; it can only be accessed through the doorway we just used. Therefore, you can stop looking around like a chump."

I'm not entirely sure what a "chump" is, but based on Leroy's grimace, it isn't a good thing. I might have known Leroy for less than a day, but I'd bet my life that he's been the Golden Boy in every classroom he's ever stepped foot in. A teacher calling him a chump is probably akin to my mom calling a cockroach cuddly.

"Does the doorway always lead here?" I ask, bracing for an insult.

"It does. Usually when you pass through the veil you will be transported to wherever you ask to go, but this door is different. It always comes straight here."

Mister Zilla explains how in the days right before graduation, he'll teach us how to locate thinnings in the veil—the spots that act as passageways between the Spirit Realm and the Land of the Living—but my brain is too busy buzzing to pay attention to anything he says after that. And from the look on Jade's face, I can tell her brain is buzzing too.

The teachers must be using one of these thin spots as

a doorway to get back to their kids, their grandkids, and their great-grandkids in the Land of the Living. Which means all we need to do is find their doorway, and we'll be set! We'll be able to sneak out and visit our families any time we want!

Only problem is, Mister Zilla won't teach us how to detect a thinning in the veil for another five years, and we don't know what to look for. Do they all shimmer like the one to Room B8? Or do some look different?

I can only guess that the search will not be easy.

But that doesn't mean I'm not going to try.

10

Elephants and Rabbits and a Dog Named Benjin

After our Introduction to Electives class—which is taught by a teacher who looks *exactly* like an oversized Q-tip (super tall, super skinny, with a mountain of curly white hair piled upon his head and pouring out of his ears and nose)—it's free time at last.

"Let's get started on our homework," Leroy suggests. His eyes dance at the idea.

It's a struggle to keep a straight face, but somehow I manage. "No thanks. I'm going exploring. But you can come along if you want."

Leroy gnaws at his bottom lip.

"Remember what Madam Booth said? Now that we've started classes, we're allowed to roam around inside the school during the day. You won't be breaking any rules."

As Leroy considers his options, Jade glides over. "That sounds fun. Can I join you?"

"Of course. And you can come too, Kevin."

Kevin looks almost horrified by the suggestion. "Nah, I prefer being by myself."

In the end, Jade's excitement rubs off on Leroy, and the three of us head out of the classroom together. With no clear destination in mind, we turn left to see where it will take us. We pass lots of portraits, but not one shimmering doorway.

Jade comes to a stop in front of a painting of a circus. There are elephants, clowns on stilts, a ringmaster holding a tall, black hat. "Do you really see things moving in the pictures? Like see them, see them?"

"Uh-huh. And you really don't?"

Jade shakes her head sadly. "I wish. Say, is there anything moving in this one?"

As I take in the swirls of red and green and blue, *everything* starts to wobble and shift. The clowns teeter across the canvas. The elephants trumpet. The ringmaster calls out to passersby, luring them into the giant red tent behind him.

"It's *all* moving."

For the next several minutes, I describe everything I see. Leroy and Jade respond perfectly: with a whole string of gasps and whoas and at least one golly geez.

Then Jade pulls me toward a portrait of a cruel-looking man holding a puppy. I narrate the scene as the dog licks the old geezer's cheek and the man's entire face cracks into a smile, his grumpiness melting away like ice cream on a hot summer day. "Good boy, Benjin," the man says in a gravelly voice as he scratches the puppy between the ears.

Next, we pause in front of a family of rabbits hopping around in a field of green. A gentle breeze wafts out of the picture, smelling like clover. And sunshine. And the park a few blocks from my house.

If I squint hard enough, I can almost pretend I see the soccer field and the slides and the swing set way off in the distance. I can almost pretend I hear Madison begging Dad to push her "higher, higher, higher!" on the swings. I can almost pretend that if I take a few steps forward, I can be reunited with my family.

Suddenly struck with inspiration, my right hand inches toward the painting. If I can *see* things in the pictures that nobody else can see, what's to say I can't slip into them too? Like a real-life Mary Poppins jumping into one of Bert's chalk drawings, could the pictures be my ticket out of Phantom Academy?

Hope flutters in my stomach as my trembling fingers close in on their target.

Please don't be solid. Please don't be solid. Please don't be solid.

It's solid.

The fluttering hope morphs into a rock the size of Alaska.

"I *think* I see your hair moving in the breeze," Jade observes, "but I wish I could feel the wind too."

I force myself to shake off my despair. Self-pity will not get me home.

Leroy and Jade keep peppering me with questions about what I see, what I hear, what I smell. As eager as they are, though, I can tell they aren't 100 percent buying what I tell them. And really, I can't blame them. I wouldn't believe it either if I didn't see the moving pictures with my own eyes.

"Hey, tell us more about when that ghost caught you talking to the painting earlier today," Jade says.

"Oh, yeah. That was scary." I relay the whole story, including how annoyed, or irritated, or angry, or *something*, the ghost—Mister Zilla—had seemed when he saw me standing in front of Mustache Lady's portrait. And how quickly Josephine had zipped her lips when she saw him approach.

"Do you think Mister Zilla believed you? When you said you were talking to yourself?" Leroy asks.

"Truthfully, I'm not sure."

"Is there anything special about Josephine's picture?" Jade asks. "You know, compared to all the others."

I think about this for a minute and decide that yes, that portrait *is* special. Of the dozens of pictures I've seen, most are like watching a movie. The characters go on about their business as though I'm not there.

Several have interacted with me by giving me directions. Or waving at me. Or—in the case of a little girl dressed in yellow-and-white striped pajamas—sticking their tongue out at me.

But Josephine Cunningham is the only one who clearly wants to tell me something important. She doesn't just smile or wave or point. She wants me to *go out* somewhere.

"She wants you to go out where?" Jade asks after I explain all this to her and Leroy.

"No clue. We keep getting interrupted before she can say more."

Leroy scratches his chin. "Does she seem mad when she says it? Maybe she wants you to get out of her school?"

"Yeah, maybe she has something against kids with freckles." Jade grins, causing dimples to form in her light brown, 100-percent-freckle-free cheeks.

I picture the expression on Josephine's face during each of our interactions. "No, she didn't look mad. More . . . eager? Plus she always calls me 'young sir.' I don't think she'd call me that if she was mad."

"Weird." Jade looks between me and the nearest painting, which is of yet another farmyard. This one doesn't have a farmer in it, or a pen full of clucking chickens, but there are leaping goats, baaing sheep, mud-caked pigs, and—unfortunately—all the usual less-than-pleasant farm aromas. "Your whole thing with the paintings is *so* weird."

"Not as weird as us being ghosts," I counter.

As Jade and I argue over where these two things fall on the weirdness scale, Leroy remains silent. Finally, he jumps back into the conversation. "Do you think Josephine wants you to go out to the school grounds? Maybe she left something out there centuries ago and she wants you to find it."

"I guess that's possible . . ."

"Or maybe," Jade butts in, "Josephine is a budding poet and 'Go Out' is the title of her latest masterpiece. But really, we could be guessing all night. Why don't we simply go to her painting right now and Finn can ask—"

I nod, even as the dinner bell cuts Jade off. "Let's go right after dinner."

But by the time we finish watching Kevin gleefully polish off his supper, and my supper, and Rebecca's supper, and we get to Josephine's frame, she's sleeping. Again! Which means Leroy finally gets his wish, and we pull out our homework.

Leroy eagerly attacks his history book, but Mister Gruber gave us three whole days to read the first chapter, and no way am I doing anything before I have to. So instead, I focus on the one assignment that's due tomorrow. Our writing assignment: Describe your favorite childhood memory. Two pages minimum.

It takes mere seconds for me to decide what I'm writing about. The best week of my entire life—by far—was when Grandma and Grandpa Winters took my family on a cruise last spring. I begin my essay by describing the ship, our teeny-tiny stateroom, the kids' club. Writing this part is easy.

Then I talk about how Grandpa and I snuck out of our rooms at exactly eleven o'clock every night to eat ice cream on the lido deck while watching the stars. Writing this part is hard.

Next, I describe how Madison would wiggle with

excitement every time I agreed to swim in the pool with her. Writing this part is really hard.

And finally, I *start* telling the story of how my mom signed her, Dad, and me up to go zip-lining, even though she's terrified of heights. How she screamed herself hoarse and almost peed her pants on the itty-bitty practice zip line, and yet she finished the entire course anyway, because she knew how much *I* wanted to do it.

Writing this part is not easy.

Writing this part is not hard.

Writing this part is not really hard.

Writing this part is impossible. Like a colossal corkscrew to the heart.

I wad up my essay and toss it across the room, where it *twacks* against the rim of the trash can and falls to the floor. I don't bother picking it up. Instead, I pull out a new sheet of paper and set to work writing about a whole new memory.

A memory with made-up parents. With a made-up brother. With a made-up puppy named Benjin.

It might be fake, but at least this memory doesn't make me want to scream. Or punch the wall. Or crumple into a ball and never move again.

This memory doesn't fill my mind with *what ifs*. And *why mes*. And a whole lot of *I just want to go homes*!

11

The Not-So-Sunny Outdoors

After a night of tossing and turning and missing my family, I'm a mess. It sure is a good thing that ghosts look the same day after day, or I'd have a case of bedhead even worse than Kevin's.

On the bright side, by the time I crawl out of bed, I've come up with three ways in which Jade and I—and hopefully Leroy—can look for an exit out of Phantom Academy:

1. We can explore every corner of the school, looking for shimmering doorways.
2. We can sneak outside and try to get through

the iron gate. Maybe there will be a thinning in the veil just outside the school grounds.
3. We can follow a teacher around at night and see where they go. If we're lucky, they'll lead us straight to a portal!

Eager to meet up with Jade in the cafeteria so we can start plotting, my fingers tap impatiently as I wait for Leroy. How a ghost who doesn't have to brush their teeth or change their clothes or even comb their hair can take so long to get ready is beyond me.

At last Leroy grabs his history book (of which the overachiever has already read four chapters) and opens our door, revealing a wide-awake Mustache Lady!

I rush outside, eager to finally learn where she wants me to go, but Leroy shakes his head. "We'd better keep moving, unless you want a repeat of yesterday."

That's when I notice the three ghosts loitering in the main corridor, in full sight of Josephine's painting. They're whispering and giggling and showing absolutely no sign of moving along any time soon.

I consider talking to Mustache Lady anyway, but Leroy nudges me forward. Our talk will have to wait.

Rather than letting myself feel disappointed, I push

Josephine Cunningham completely out of my mind. I need to focus on my main goal: escape.

"Okay, you two," I say as soon as Leroy and I park ourselves next to Jade at Table Eight. "I have a plan. When morning announcements are over, let's slip outside." I keep my voice low in case this breaks a school rule—or two or three school rules. "We can scout the school grounds and see if there is any way past that stone wall."

"I'm in," Jade says immediately. "I could do with an adventure."

We both look at Leroy, who's staring intently at his fingernails—even though they've been the exact same length, the exact same color, and have been surrounded by the exact same hangnails for the past three months.

"I don't think we're allowed to go outside," he says finally. "So I'll stay here, just in case."

Jade's eyes light up. "Oh, that's so nice of you, Leroy. If anyone comes looking for us, you can say we're in the bathroom or something."

I can tell from Leroy's expression that being our cover *had not* been his objective at all, but he nods anyway. "I can do that."

Madam Booth's announcements take all of two minutes, and then Jade and I spring to our feet and drift speedily—

but not so speedily that we look suspicious—past the staff table. Amazingly, nobody says a word. The cafeteria isn't far from the school's entrance, which means that in no time at all we're pushing open the heavy front door.

"Man, I've wandered around inside the school after lights out several times, but I haven't had the guts to come out here until now. I miss being outside so much! I miss digging in the dirt, dancing in the rain, even the smell of sunscreen." Jade is practically skipping as we head down the same gravel path that Madam Booth and I used on my first day as a ghost.

It's hard to believe that walk occurred less than forty-eight hours ago. It feels like an eternity has passed since I got clobbered by a coconut and decided to take the trail through the woods.

"Say, Jade? Do you ever wish you'd taken the other path when you died? The one that went through the field of flowers?"

Jade thinks long and hard before she answers.

"When I first got here, I regretted my choice a lot. But then I realized I have no clue where the other path goes. Maybe everyone who went that way has to clean toilets all day. Or maybe they're stuck inside a hot, stuffy, overcrowded shopping mall that only sells rotten fruit. Or what if they're all sitting in a concert hall, listening to Mozart songs being played on out-of-tune violins?"

"Or maybe they're waiting in a line that never, ever ends," I add, shuddering at the thought. Waiting in line is bad enough, but waiting in line while *also* standing next to my Great-Aunt Edna? Talk about torture!

"Exactly! So eventually, I decided to stop second-guessing my pick; it does no good."

"Wow, you're really smart."

Jade laughs a tinkling kind of laugh that reminds me of my favorite teacher from Savannah Oaks. "Nah, I've just had four months to think about it."

Four months or not, I still think she's pretty smart.

I decide to follow her lead.

"The grass sure looks funny, doesn't it?" Jade observes, clearly eager to change the subject.

The ocean of green that spreads all the way from the gravel path to the stone wall does, indeed, look strange. The dusky, sage-colored blades are way thinner and pokier than any grass I've ever seen before. It's as though they were painted onto the ground with an ultra-fine-tipped paintbrush and some not-quite-right green paint.

"Yeah, and the sky looks weird too." There's an unsettling orange tint to it, like someone smeared cantaloupe puree all over the blue. There isn't a single cloud in sight either. And no sun, for that matter.

After giving ourselves a moment to digest our normal-not-normal surroundings, Jade and I plow ahead to the iron gate. I give it a tug, pulling on it with all my weight, but the thing will not open.

"Let's check the wall," Jade suggests.

We march along it, looking for any shimmery portals concealed within its surface. We find a great big diddly-squat. The school grounds likewise look about as boring as boring can be. Apart from a large garden behind the school, our view from the wall reveals nothing but grass, and grass, and yet more sage-colored grass.

Eventually we arrive back at the gate, and I give it a frustrated kick. "I sure hope the thinning in the veil the teachers use is somewhere inside Phantom Academy, because I don't think we're getting off school grounds without a key."

"I wonder if all the teachers have a key, or if Madam Booth's the only one," Jade muses aloud. "Maybe we can take one while a teacher is distracted?"

"Oh, that's an idea!" I've never stolen anything in my life—not counting the occasional candy from Mom's hidden stash, which she thought I didn't know about—but things are different now. I'm locked in a school, for cripes sake. If stealing is the only way I can get back to my family, well then, *hello life of crime.*

Jade shakes her head, sending her rainbow-colored hair swishing from side to side. "No, Finn. Forget I mentioned the key, okay? I was merely thinking out loud. I didn't mean it."

"But what if—"

"No, Finn!" she repeats, this time more forcefully. "You know I'm all for sneaking around and stuff, but this is *stealing* we're talking about. What if we're caught? I doubt the Spirit Realm has a juvie system. We'd probably be forced to move on."

Eek. I definitely do not want to be moved on. "You're right. We'll have to be super careful to make sure we aren't caught, and—"

"Finn, I said forget it. Even if we get past this gate, we'll have no idea what to do next. I mean, look out there." She gestures through a gap between two iron bars. As far as I can see there is nothing but miles and miles of hills and valleys and trees.

"We can at least try going back to where we first met Madam Booth. We entered the Spirit Realm there, so maybe we can leave it from there too."

It seems like the perfect idea, but Jade shakes her head

again. "It's a good thought, but when I first got here, I asked Madam Booth if I could change my mind and go back. But she said the gateway I'd just come through was one-way only."

I let out the world's biggest sigh.

"Why don't we forget about the gate and check out the garden quick?" Jade says. "We probably have twenty minutes before class starts, and maybe we'll find something interesting."

"I guess..." I reluctantly fall into step behind Jade as she heads around back. As I walk, though, I remember Leroy's theory about Josephine Cunningham: maybe she wants me to find something she left out on the school grounds centuries ago.

Maybe this outdoor adventure is salvageable, after all.

I pick up my pace.

Soon we're leaving the dusky grass behind and entering the garden, which is a virtual jungle of twiggy bushes, eggplant-purple vines, and shoulder-high plants bearing heart-shaped fruits the color of boogers. There are trees with bloodred leaves, shrubs covered in tiny yellow thorns, and a row of plants teeming with pumpkin-orange vegetables that smell almost as bad as my gym socks.

Like a dog drawn to another dog's butt, Jade rockets

toward a woody plant blanketed in iridescent beetles the size of golf balls. "These are incredible!" She taps one of the beetles gently on the back, and it buzzes angrily before zooming off. "What I wouldn't give for some colored pencils and my field journal."

"You might want to draw one, but I want to stash one in a certain kid's lunch box." (I'm talking about you, Lucas McGreedy, from Miss Granger's homeroom class at Savannah Oaks. *You're* that kid.)

"If it weren't so cruel to the beetles, I'd dearly love to shove a couple of these beauties into the toe of one of my hermana María's knockoff designer shoes. She was the worst!"

I head deeper into the greenery, leaving Jade behind to get acquainted with her new insect friends. There's no doubt that the garden is cool in a creepy kind of way, but I don't see anything that looks like it could have been left out here an eternity ago by Mustache Lady. There isn't a single treasure chest with Josephine's name scrawled across the lid. No tree bearing a hollowed-out cavity in which some precious artifact could have been stashed. No neon sign saying, DIG HERE TO FIND JOSEPHINE CUNNINGHAM'S STUFF.

After five or so minutes of lifting boulders and peeking under salmon-colored leaves the size of volleyballs, I grudgingly return to Jade, who's now sitting crisscross applesauce above the dirt.

"Check this out." She points excitedly to an insect that looks like a supersized purple grasshopper. "How are there living plants and insects in the Spirit Realm, do you think? I would have thought everything here would be dead, like us."

She's got me stumped there. "I'm not sure, but we should probably head back inside."

Out of habit, my eyes flit toward the watch on my wrist. 3:28 p.m.

It said the same exact time yesterday morning. And last night. And earlier today. But even though my watch hasn't worked since the moment I died, I can still tell that our time is running short. And Madam Booth will no doubt skin us alive if we don't make it to class on time.

"Yeah, you're probably right." Jade crawls to her feet, pushes up on her glasses, and lets out an irritated grunt when they remain stubbornly fixed in place. Like always. "Let's go."

We circle back to the front door, and I yank down on the handle. The thing doesn't budge! I try again, but it's no use.

Jade shoves me out of the way and tries herself, as though maybe in my twelve years of life I somehow never mastered the skill of opening a door, but of course she's no more successful than I was. The door is every bit as impenetrable as Phantom Academy's iron gate.

Jade and I are locked outside.

12

I Spill the Beans

Jade yanks on the door a few more times before throwing up her arms in frustration. "Maybe there's a window we can sneak through. Or wasn't there another door near the garden? Maybe it's unlocked."

I don't have any better ideas, so we take off around the school, checking windows as we go. The first one is sealed up tight. So is the second. And the third. And the fourth. Panic is setting in big-time when Jade gestures toward Phantom Academy's towering back wall. At first I'm not sure what she's pointing at, but then I see it. A door, almost completely hidden behind a curtain of ivy.

"This had better be unlocked," I murmur as I reach for the doorknob.

Just as my fingertips touch the cool metal, the door swings outward, nearly smacking me in the face. I stumble backward as *something* whooshes past. A brown, waist-high something that's almost instantly swallowed up by the overgrown garden.

I frantically scan the tangle of plants, but the only browns I see come in the form of creeping tree roots and bushy shrubs. The *thing* is nowhere to be seen.

"Umm, Finn? What was that?" Jade sputters.

I have to swallow a couple of times before I'm able to speak. "I have no idea." I scan the garden again—

left,

right,

left—

but nothing looks out of place. "At least the door is still cracked open. Let's go!"

"But what if the ghost is still in there? Someone must have let that thing outside, right? You never even turned the doorknob!"

Rotten radishes, I hadn't thought of that. But if I have to choose between facing Madam Booth's wrath for being late to class or encountering some unknown ghost who sets ominous, brown, streaking things loose in the garden, I'm picking the unknown ghost who sets ominous, brown, streaking things loose in the garden. No question about it.

I tiptoe to the door, peak through the gap, and find myself looking into a kitchen. A kitchen that clearly hasn't seen an upgrade in at least one hundred years. There isn't a single electric oven or refrigerator or fancy-schmancy appliance in sight.

Dozens of cast-iron pots and pans hang from a rack above an open hearth. Shelves overflow with an odd assortment of glass jars, each one filled with a brown or green or yellow powder. There are ceramic containers holding wooden spatulas and stirring spoons, a row of dusty cookbooks that look like they've never been opened, and off in a corner is a huge mound of the heart-shaped, booger-colored fruits from the garden. Bundles of garlic-like bulbs and wheat-like stalks dangle from the ceiling, and every time I turn my head, my nose is blasted with smells—most of which remind me of vomit or pig poo.

At least the room is free of cobwebs.

And ghosts.

"Let's go, quick, before the cook—or that brown thingy—come back," I whisper.

We race through the kitchen and find ourselves right

back in the cafeteria, where the grandfather clock displays a time of 8:58 a.m. We have two minutes to make it to Room 11 or our afterlives are over!

Jade and I take off down the hall, whipping around corners and almost taking out a ten-foot-tall statue of a minotaur before sliding into our seats, mere seconds before the bell rings.

Ghosts might not need to breathe, but this doesn't stop me from panting and wheezing like I'd run a marathon. And my heart, which I'm pretty sure has no *actual* blood to pump, feels like it's going a mile a minute.

"Finally," Leroy hisses.

"Sorry, we had a few problems getting back in. The door . . ." My voice trails off as I notice the peeved expression on Madam Booth's face. The pointy toe of her left shoe taps impatiently—and soundlessly—an inch above the ground.

"If Finn is ready for us to start class, let's begin."

All through reading and writing classes, I can't stop thinking about two things. (And no. They are not reading *or* writing.)

First, there's the brown, streaking *something*. Like seriously, what was that? The Spirit Realm's ghostly version of a Chupacabra, perhaps?

And second, there's everything else Jade and I found outside. Or rather, everything we *didn't* find, like a way off campus or anything that looked like it could have been left out there by Josephine. Our whole "adventure" had turned into nothing but an hour of failure and fear, all rolled into one. And if anything, I'm even farther away from finding a way out of the school than I was when I first woke up. Because now I know that without a key, the school grounds—and whatever lays beyond—are a great big dead end.

When Mister Gruber enters the room for history class and announces that "Today, we'll be discussing the anatomy of Phantom Academy itself," I figure I'll have yet another hour of boredom to fill with daydreams about Chupacabras and shimmering doorways.

But boredom and daydreaming are not what I get.

First Mister Gruber explains how the school's walls and floors and doorframes are not made from the wood of an oak or maple or elm tree. They're made from Ghoul trees, a species that thrives in the Spirit Realm despite the lack of rain or sunlight. Apparently, they can tower hundreds of feet in the air!

Then he tells us the fires that burn in Phantom Academy's fireplaces are not yellow or orange or red like they are in the Land of the Living. They're purple!

"And all the windows in the school are for appearances only," he continues. "None of them open or close. This is because—"

"Wait! What?" Leroy the Rule Follower doesn't even raise his hand before he interrupts Mister Gruber midsentence. "The windows don't open? Are you saying there's only one way out of this room?"

Mister Gruber nods, and Leroy rapidly falls to pieces. He clutches his chest, looks frantically around the classroom, and starts sputtering on and on about fire safety and building codes and evacuation plans and sprinkler systems and Phantom Academy's disturbing lack of smoke alarms.

Soon you'd think Leroy was being chased by Godzilla, he's hyperventilating so much, and he doesn't calm down until Mister Gruber finally succeeds in shushing him long enough to deliver a rather humorous lecture on how ghosts are *not actually flammable*.

It's an entertaining ten minutes for sure, and better yet, Leroy's outburst gives me a great idea.

I raise my hand.

"Mister Gruber, sir? What if there is an *actual* emergency in the Spirit Realm, though, and we need to evacuate to the Land of the Living? Does the school have a way for us to get there?" My fingers *rap, rap, rap* against my desk as I wait for his answer.

"An emergency?" Mister Gruber's forehead scrunches, like he's unsure what kind of emergency would require us to vacate the place in a hurry. Does the Spirit Realm not have natural disasters like earthquakes or tidal waves or volcanoes? I'm beginning to think my question will be yet another dead end when Mister Gruber's eyes light up. "Oh, you mean like if the Three Hundred and Ninety-Second Ghost War were to break out tomorrow?"

My mouth gapes open. There have been over three *hundred* ghost wars?! Mister Gruber had better not be planning to teach us about ALL of them! But at least these wars give me just the "emergency" I need. "Yes, that's exactly what I mean. What will happen then?"

"I don't think another war is likely any time soon, little ghostling. We've had almost fifty years of peace since the Binding Nonaggression Treaty of Complete and Continuous Cooperation was signed at the end of the Three Hundred and Ninety-First Ghost War. The experts believe this treaty could last for centuries."

"Oh, I know all about that treaty, sir," I lie, "but another war is still something I worry about. A lot." I try my best to mirror Leroy's terrified expression from five minutes ago.

"If the Three Hundred and"—I mumble a few random, unintelligible words under my breath—"Ghost War did break out tomorrow, could we escape? Could we leave the Spirit Realm quickly enough?"

"That truly isn't something you need to concern yourself with, but to put your mind at ease, yes. We are only a mile from the nearest thinning in the veil, excluding the one leading to Room B8, of course. We could all evacuate fairly quickly."

A look of horror crosses Jade's face. "A mile?" she mouths in my direction. My eyes start to prickle, and I thank my Lucky Charms that ghosts can't cry. A mile is far worse than my worst fears. Even if Jade and I somehow make it past the gate, how will we ever find something that far away?

My family feels farther away than ever.

Mister Gruber must mistake my despair for mounting fear, because he gives me what I suspect is intended to be a reassuring smile (but which *actually* makes it look like he's suffering from a horrendous case of hemorrhoids). "Really and truly, there is no need for you to concern yourself with these matters anymore. There is no imminent war. And even if there were, it would take more than a simple skirmish for the headmaster to call for an evacuation. One shudders to think of the consequences of having untrained ghosts anywhere near the Living. Now *that* would be a true nightmare!"

Mister Gruber looks around the room at all of us "untrained ghosts" and shakes his head. But what, exactly, does he think we'd do? We can't even pick up a book yet; we're about as far from a threat as you can get!

"Now let's leave all this silly war talk behind us and get back to our lecture. Has anyone noticed any other unusual features of Phantom Academy?"

I'm too busy contemplating my five-year prison sentence—the one that increasingly seems to come with no hope of escape or parole—to register his last question. It isn't until the silence drags on that I finally process Mister Gruber's words.

Well, yes. As a matter of fact, I *have* noticed unusual things. The paintings here all move and talk and fart, and I'm apparently the only one who notices.

Or am I?

My slumped-over back unslumps itself as I'm struck with yet another idea. Just because my classmates can't see or hear anything move in the canvases doesn't mean nobody else can. What if there are others, and not just those with freckles or hazel eyes? My memory flashes back to the day

I saw Mister Zilla in front of Josephine's painting. What if he wasn't talking to himself after all?

And not only that, what if my ability actually *means* something? Like maybe people who can communicate with oil paintings and watercolors are considered special, and they all get to leave school early!

Before I can think too hard, I raise my hand.

Somewhere in the deep recesses of my brain, I hear Mom's voice spouting her favorite mantra—*Think before you act, Finn!*—but I'm too excited *and too desperate* for her words to do any good.

Not that her mantra ever did all that much good...

"You again?" Mister Gruber grumbles once it's clear nobody else is about to raise their hand. "Go ahead."

"The paintings here are unusual. The people and animals in them can move."

The look that crosses Mister Gruber's face is almost comical. His eyeballs double in size. His jaw goes slack. And his eyebrows arch until they look like my mom's back when she does the cat pose in yoga. "You see the paintings...*move?*" he finally asks, his voice so quiet I can hardly hear it over Rebecca's giggles.

I nod, ignoring the clanking sound coming from the beads in Leroy's braids as he frantically shakes his head, signaling me to stay quiet. I can't give up hope yet. "I do. And many of them talk, too. Like Josephine Cunningham clearly wants to tell me something. I just haven't figured out what it is yet."

Mister Gruber begins pacing across the room,
back and forth,
back and forth,
back and forth.

"When the academy was first built," he says eventually, "Josephine was rumored to have been able to talk to the paintings. But nobody else has ever had that particular talent, so it's long been assumed she was faking it. But now..."

Mister Gruber resumes his pacing. And I resume my earlier slumped posture. All my great ideas today are turning into big fat nothings.

"I'm sure Finn is faking it too," Rebecca says as she aims a sneer in my direction.

"Yeah, I agree with Rebecca," Leroy the Traitor pipes in. "You should ignore everything he said."

I glare at Leroy, but he's too busy staring straight ahead to notice.

Several minutes tick by before Mister Gruber clears his throat. "If you aren't joking, Finn, if you truly can talk to the paintings, especially *that* painting, then I implore you to ignore everything Josephine Cunningham tells you." His eyes bore into mine. "Everyone knows that woman is *not* to be trusted."

13

I Do the Unthinkable

As soon as we're back in the cafeteria after history class, I round on Leroy.

"Why did you side with Rebecca before?" I hiss, keeping my voice low enough that only Leroy and Jade can hear. Not that Kevin would have noticed anyway. He's *way* too preoccupied with his lunch, a bowl of slimy, pale yellow goo that looks like it was mined from the nostril of an ogre. "You know I can talk to the paintings, but you made me sound like a liar!"

"I'm sorry, but I was trying to help. I'm not sure you should be telling the teachers—or other students, for that matter—about your . . . skill? Your gift? Whatever it is. I think you should keep it quiet, at least for now. At least until we've learned more about it."

His eyes, which are so dark they're almost black, beg me to understand.

"Maybe you're right." I groan. Why does being a ghost have to be so complicated? "But I wonder why Mister Gruber reacted the way he did to me saying that Josephine Cunningham wanted to talk to me. What did she do to make everyone turn against her so much?"

I've always hated bullies, and it seems to me like the entire ghost world is bullying her. Mustache Lady has always seemed nice to me, even if she is a little over sleepy.

Leroy glances at the clock. "We've still got forty minutes before our next class. Let's see what we can find out about her in the library."

Now normally I'd reject any plan that meant walking into a library *on purpose*, but my desire for information is apparently greater than my dislike for books. I agree to the unthinkable.

Leroy, Jade, and I dump our ogre boogers into Kevin's bowl and head toward the hallway. Leroy leads the way, of course; he's the only one who knows where to go.

As we pass the staff table, I notice that Mister Gruber and Mister Zilla are deep in conversation. They're so intense, you'd think they were discussing the meaning of death. Then all at once, their eyes flicker my way—all four of them—and my throat squeezes.

There's no doubt in my mind that they're talking about me. Me and my little I-can-speak-to-the-paintings revelation.

Any lingering shred of hope that my "ability" could somehow earn me a free pass home is long gone now, because neither teacher looks happy. Mister Gruber is all frowny faced and stiff jawed while Mister Zilla has gone back to channeling his inner Darth Sidious.

I shiver and squeeze in closer to Leroy as we float out of the room. A few twists and turns later, we arrive at our destination, where all thoughts of terrifying teachers and recklessly spilled secrets are forced right out of my head.

Because the Phantom Academy library?

It's majorly WOW!

The circular room, which must be housed in one of the school's towers, is at least forty feet tall. Every square inch of wall space, for as high as I can see, is covered in leather-bound books. Huge, movable ladders are placed every few feet to give access to each and every title. In the middle of the room is a massive, round fireplace surrounded by darkly stained Ghoul-wood tables. The place smells like paper, charcoal, and dust, with a hint of nutmeg.

If all libraries looked and smelled like this one, even *I* might be tempted to take up reading.

The only thing I can think to complain about is the fireplace, which is sadly unlit. There's not a single purple flame in sight.

While Jade and I spin in circles, taking everything in, Leroy beelines it toward a cabinet filled with tiny drawers. Eventually, I stop my gawking and tag along.

"What is this?" Jade asks as she drums her knuckles against the cabinet.

"A card catalog. It's how libraries were organized back before computers were invented." Leroy flips through the hundreds of index cards filed away inside one of the drawers. "I'd ask Madam Penn to point us in the right direction," he says, nodding to a ghost sitting behind a large desk, "but I'm not sure we should advertise what we're looking for."

Not that Madam Penn looks like she'd be much help anyway. Her attention hasn't deviated from the book on her desk since we first entered the room.

After digging around a while longer, Leroy lets out a shout of triumph. "I found something!"

"Leroy, shhhhh!" Jade whispers, her finger pressed to her lips. "We're in a *library!*"

A look of horror crosses Leroy's face, and Jade bursts out laughing. "I'm only kidding. I don't think Madam Penn has even noticed we're here yet. I'm pretty sure we can be as loud as we want."

Despite Jade's reassurances, Leroy silently motions for me to hand him a tiny pencil and a slip of paper from off the miniature table in front of me. Then he jots something down: 930.092 VICTO.

I vaguely recall learning about book numbers like this back when I was in living-people school. Was it the Huey decimal system? The Dewey decimal system? The Louie decimal system? I can't remember; I've never needed to use it.

Leroy studies the shelves before pointing to a spot at least twenty feet above our heads. "It should be up there. Ugh, *of course* it's way up there." His voice trembles slightly as he moves a ladder into position.

"I'll grab it," Jade volunteers. "Heights don't bother me one bit. I used to climb trees all the time, looking for insects."

Leroy gives Jade a quick lesson on the Dewey decimal system (I *knew* it was one of the ducks!), and in no time at all she's racing up the ladder like a squirrel. She comes back down a few moments later with a gigantic tome cradled under her right arm. The words "*Phantom Academy: Its Early Days* by Scott Victor" are stamped across the front in gold letters.

We plop down at the table farthest away from Madam Penn—who is still captivated by whatever she's reading—and Leroy opens the book to the index. He scans the text and flips to a page featuring a giant picture of Mustache Lady, sitting by a piano. The three of us crowd together and read.

> *Josephine Cunningham was born in London, England, in 1685. She joined her brother, Sir Arthur George Cunningham III, on his 1705 voyage to America. Josephine never married and never had children. She embarked on her journey to the next life in 1725.*

"'Embarked on her journey to the next life?'" Jade scoffs. "What a ridiculous way to say she croaked."

> *Upon their deaths, Josephine and Sir Arthur worked intimately together to build*

and design Phantom Academy. By all accounts, they had an amicable relationship, except surrounding the issue of doorways through the veil. Josephine fervently believed students should have periodic access to the Land of the Living, arguing that the ability to see the greater world would ease their transition into ghosthood and make for a smoother adjustment to life after graduation.

Sir Arthur maintained that the school must be kept closed. He did not trust the young students to act appropriately and ventured they would draw too much attention.

As construction on the academy drew to an end, their disagreement over access to the veil did not. Exactly one year after Phantom Academy opened its doors, Josephine Cunningham disappeared. She has not been seen or heard from since.

By the time we reach the bottom of the page, my heart is full of warmth toward Mustache Lady—who was clearly the good gal in all this—and a burning, hot hatred toward her brother.

"This is intense," Jade says. "I don't think I like this Sir Arthur dude very much."

Ditto, Jade. Diiiitto!

"So it's Sir Arthur's fault I can't see my parents." Leroy's face is a virtual kaleidoscope of sadness and anger and frustration. I'd laugh, but my face probably looks the same. If Josephine had gotten her way, I'd probably have been able to visit my family by now.

I'd know if Madison has forgiven me for not waking up.

I'd know if Cecelia LaGrange got voted out of grandma's knitting circle for daring to crochet when she should have been knitting.

I'd know if my mom has remembered how to breathe.

The weight of it all is too much. My heart hurts. My head pounds. And my fingers itch to rip Sir Arthur George Cunningham III's portrait down from its place of honor on the first-floor landing and toss it unceremoniously onto one of Phantom Academy's purple fires.

A roar bubbles up in my throat, but before it can erupt, I notice that a new emotion has taken over the kaleidoscope on Leroy's face: determination.

"I'm in," Leroy says, his voice flat, but firm.

"You're what?" Jade's head tilts, which actually makes her glasses appear straight for once.

"Your plot to escape. I'm in."

Jade's face lights up. "Really? That's great!" She lifts her hand for a high five, and Leroy slaps his palm to hers. Instead of the usual satisfying *smack*, their ghostly high five sounds more like a blobfish squelching onto the deck of a ship. Not that this diminishes our enthusiasm at all. I give them each a squelchy, blobfishy high five of my own.

As Leroy glances over at Madam Penn to make sure we're not in trouble for high-fiving in the library (we aren't; she still hasn't looked up), I assess my new partners in crime. Jade and Leroy are nothing like my real-world friends, who were only interested in soccer and gaming and goofing off. Instead, they're clever and kind and weird, all in equal measure.

And the three of us?

We're breaking out of Alcatraz!

14

A Cat Smokes a Pipe

After Jade returns *Phantom Academy: Its Early Days* to its home in the nosebleed section of the library, we head out the door. My thoughts remain focused on escape plans as we float down the hallway, but Leroy—being Leroy—has gone back to pondering what we'd just read.

"I wonder what happened to Josephine. Scott Victor wrote that she 'disappeared,' but do you think she left on her own? Or did her brother force her away?"

Jade shrugs, but I know how we can find the answer. "Come free time, we're talking to Josephine." Mustache

Lady might be three-fourths sloth, but I'm not letting some closed eyes stop me this time.

We arrive in Room 11 almost ten minutes before BTBGYCB class is due to start, so Madam Lecter takes it upon herself to entertain us with hilarious stories about her family. The second the bell rings, though, her lecturing begins.

And I zone out.

All the questions I want to ask Josephine float through my head. Questions like:

Where does she want me to go?

Where is the real Mustache Lady now? The one that isn't trapped inside a painting?

Was her mean big brother the one who forced her to go away?

Can she shed any light on the school's brown, streaking, Chupacabra problem? (Leroy is convinced Jade and I imagined the whole thing, but I'm not buying that for a second.)

And finally, does the school have a gate key hidden somewhere, like how my parents keep a spare house key stashed inside a fake rock? And if we *do* get past the gate, which way should we turn? Is the nearest thinning of the veil a mile to the left? To the right? Straight ahead?

As a cofounder of the school, Josephine Cunningham is sure to have all the answers. Isn't she?

Somehow I make it through BTBGYCB class, Haunting 101, *and* Intro to Electives class without being eaten alive by my own impatience. But when free time finally arrives, I'm off. Jade and Leroy can hardly keep up as I speed toward Mustache Lady's portrait.

"You know it's possible she won't have all the answers we're looking for," Leroy says, his voice coming out in gasps. "The Josephine in the painting might only know about things that happened *before* she was painted."

Dratted donkeys, I hadn't considered that. I pick up my pace even more as I zoom up the last set of stairs—all eighteen of them—to arrive on the third floor. At last, I'm standing in front of a picture.

Only it's not the picture I'm looking for. Instead of Josephine Cunningham, I'm face-to-face with a cat.

A pipe-smoking, kiwi-eyed, orange tabby cat, to be specific.

Mustache Lady is nowhere to be seen.

"What the . . ." I mutter as the cat blows a giant smoke ring that soars right out of the picture.

"Josephine is supposed to be there, right?" Jade asks as she points at the cat, who's purring so loud it's hard to believe she and Leroy can't hear it.

I nod as I walk back to the main hallway. Where

could she have gone? She was here this morning.

"Well, *that's* suspicious," Jade mumbles as she joins the search. "Maybe you can ask one of the other pictures what happened to her."

It's a great idea, except it turns out that all the pictures nearby are of buildings or oceans or pipe-smoking cats. Not exactly key eyewitness material.

The closest portrait of a person feels like it's a mile away.

"Hello, mister," I say to a man who looks every bit as sour as I'd look if I had to sit in a stiff, hard-backed wooden chair and read the exact same book (*A Study of Sixteenth-Century Medicinal Herbs*) year after year after year. "Any chance you saw a ghost drift by, carrying a picture?"

The man grumps. "Ghosts float by me all the time. I pay them no heed."

I'm not sure I believe him; in his shoes, I'd probably be so bored that I'd happily watch *anything* drift past—even if it was just a particularly large speck of dust.

"The missing portrait is of Josephine Cunningham," I say, thinking maybe this piece of information will get him chatting. If Mustache Lady could really talk to the Phantom Academy paintings, maybe the two of them struck up a great friendship once upon a time.

But the man merely grumps again. "We do not speak of that woman."

"Why not? Why don't you speak of her?" I ask. But the man has already closed his eyes. The snores rumbling out of his frame are about as believable as Madison was that time she blamed an entire empty package of Double Stuf Oreos on Bubbles, her stuffed hippo.

"Well, he was the opposite of helpful," I complain to Jade and Leroy. "Let's keep looking. She's got to be somewhere."

Jade walks to the end of the hallway and promptly waves Leroy and me over.

"Look." She points to the left, where a ghost's bright red hair is disappearing around a corner about twenty yards away.

I don't hesitate a second. I slip into the hallway and follow the red. "That was the cook, wasn't it? Shouldn't he be downstairs? Cooking dinner?"

"Maybe he finished early and is going to his room for a quick break?" Leroy suggests.

But Jade shakes her head. "No way. I've snuck out of my room plenty of times, and I know for a fact that all the staff rooms are on the first floor."

"Was he carrying a painting, Jade?" I whisper as we near the corner where the cook disappeared.

"I don't think so, but maybe?"

Only one way to find out. I swallow hard, then leap forward like a TV cop busting into a bad guy's lair. A great big corridor of emptiness stretches out in front of me. The cook is nowhere to be seen.

"Well, fartsicle," I moan. He must have turned down another hallway, or entered a room, or taken a back staircase.

After a quick, unsuccessful hunt for the cook, we refocus on Josephine. I ask every painting of a man, woman, or child that we float past if they've noticed anything suspicious, but nobody's seen a thing.

Actually, that's not entirely true. When we get to the painting of the man on a unicycle, he looks like he might be in the know. But instead of speaking, he keeps looking over my shoulder. Like he's not sure he should be seen talking to me.

I beg him to say something, anything, but he just shakes his head and continues biking back and forth. Back and forth. Back and forth, down the country lane. Refusing to say a word.

15
Fishier than Fish Tacos

Jade, Leroy, and I whisper our way through dinner as we try to work out what could have happened to Mustache Lady. We come up with five hypotheses:

1. The cook moved her for some strange, unknown reason. That's why he was wandering around the third-floor hallways during free time.
2. It's normal for paintings to be moved from place to place. Living in a school for decade upon decade must get frightfully dull for the

teachers, so maybe they move the paintings around from time to time to keep things feeling fresh.
3. Her portrait was eaten by the brown, streaking thing that Jade and I saw in the garden. Though let's face it. The thing probably prefers a diet of underage ghosts.
4. The picture was in need of restoration. Maybe Josephine Cunningham is sitting in some portrait-fix-it-up place in the basement right now, about to get a free facelift.
5. Josephine was moved because I let it slip that her painting was trying to talk to me, and somebody didn't want that conversation to happen. Somebody was afraid of what she might tell me.

My money is on theory number five.

Jade seems to have something against the cook.

And Leroy refuses to even make a guess, given what he calls "our paucity of data." "Why don't we ask Madam Booth? She knows everything about everything. If the painting was moved because it needed repairs or as part of some hallway redesign project, surely, she'd know."

"But, Leroy, what if Madam Booth was the one who moved it?" Jade asks. "That woman thinks reading is *fun*, and I find that mighty suspicious." Her eyes fall to Leroy's READ MORE BOOKS! T-shirt and she grimaces slightly. "Except in your case, of course."

After I stop cackling at Leroy's expression, I peek up at the staff table. The black feathers on Madam Booth's hat are definitely dodgy, but she doesn't look evil otherwise. "I think Leroy's right that Madam Booth is fairly safe, but I can't say the same for the ghost next to her." Today, our reading and writing teacher is sitting right next to Mister Zilla, aka Evil Personified. "We'd better wait until tomorrow to talk to her."

Even though tomorrow feels like a lifetime away.

That night, as we lie in bed, Leroy can't seem to settle. After his fifty-seventh sigh, I ask what's up.

"I think today was my brother's birthday, and I completely forgot about it until now. I'm a terrible brother." Our bedroom might be darker than dark, but I can still feel the despair rolling off him.

"You are not a terrible brother, Leroy. I'm impressed you even know what day it is."

In a few more weeks, I'll probably forget what *month* it is; no way I'm remembering the date.

"I bet my parents let him celebrate early by taking

him to the last Frisco RoughRiders home baseball game of the season, like they did last year." Leroy sighs for the fifty-eighth time. "That was a really fun day, but I complained the entire time because they wouldn't let me bring a book along. I wish I could have a do-over on that day."

Man, if we could have do-over days, I'd redo a lot of them. Like the day I decided it was a good idea to give myself a haircut in kindergarten.

Or the day I broke my arm because Lucas McGreedy dared me to jump off the monkey bars during recess.

Or the day I told Mom I hated her because she wouldn't let me go swimming during a thunderstorm.

Or the day I decided to walk under a palm tree and—

I shake my head. If I'm not careful, soon I'll be joining Leroy in his great big gutter of gloom. It's time for a topic change.

"Madam Lecter's stories were funny today, though, weren't they? I thought Madison had a ton of blowout diapers, but she was nothing compared to Madam Lecter's kid. What did she call him again?"

Leroy lets out a chuckle. A weak one, but a chuckle nonetheless. "The Prince of Poop."

"Oh yeah. The Prince of Poop. I guess that makes Madison the Duchess of Dung."

Leroy's laugh is bigger this time, and when he finally says good night, I can hear his smile.

In the ensuing silence, I go back to pondering brown, streaky things and hidden keys and missing portraits, and by the time Leroy and I finally leave our bedroom in the morning, I've half convinced myself that Mustache Lady will be back in her frame, waiting for us. The thought that someone could have moved her picture to prevent me from talking to her feels like something out of a movie.

Surely, we imagined the whole thing.

But nope. It's the cat, not Josephine, who greets me in the hallway with a big puff of smoke. I nod politely—there's no need to be rude, after all—and drift on past.

Jade is waiting for us by the main staircase, her legs bouncing like a kangaroo. "Last night felt like it went on forever. This mystery is the most exciting thing to happen to me in forever! Apart from discovering a new species of beetle, of course, but I died before I could get any credit for that."

Now that I think about it, the same could sadly be said for me, too. Not the beetle bit, obviously, but the rest of it. As much as I miss my family and my life, it was all rather boring. There was school, soccer, homework, oodles of PlayStation playing, the occasional trip to the beach, and that was about it. Mysterious, disappearing paintings were simply not a part of my daily existence. It's all rather thrilling, actually! (Not that I wouldn't go back to my dad's cooking and family game nights and Grandma and Grandpa Winters' weekly Sunday visits in a heartbeat if I could. Because boring or not, I totally would.)

We float into the cafeteria, and Jade lets out an enthusiastic whoop. I follow her gaze to the staff table, where Madam Booth is sitting in the very last seat. Not only that, but the seat next to her is miraculously still empty. We've hit the jackpot.

Without saying a word, Leroy, Jade, and I surround her. "I will not accept any excuses for incomplete work," she says firmly. "There are no dogs at Phantom Academy to eat your homework."

While it's true that I did not finish our assigned reading last night, I wave away her words. "We aren't here to talk homework, Madam Booth. We're wondering if you know why one of the third-floor paintings was moved yesterday."

A flash of emotion—curiosity maybe, or suspicion—flashes across her face when she looks at me, but it's gone so fast that I decide I must have imagined it. "A painting was moved? How interesting."

"Doesn't that happen sometimes, though?" Leroy asks. "Don't the pictures occasionally get switched around or taken down for repairs?"

"Not in the hundred plus years I've been—"

Madam Booth's words are cut off as Madam Lecter approaches the empty chair next to her. As usual, our BTBGYCB teacher can't seem to keep the smile off her face as she takes her seat. "Sorry I'm late," she whispers to Madam Booth. "I lost track of time."

"No worries," Madam Booth replies before turning back to us, her eyes focused on Leroy. "I'm really not sure why the painting was moved."

"A painting was moved?" Madam Lecter asks as she fiddles with one of the ties coming off her hospital gown. "Which one?"

Jade quickly fills them in on how Josephine Cunningham's portrait was replaced with a cat. Madam Booth's face looks equal parts baffled and intrigued, but Madam Lecter's shoulders relax. "Oh, if it's that painting, I wouldn't worry about it. I'd bet Headmaster Cunningham was missing his family, so he moved his great-aunt's portrait into his office for a bit."

I chew on my lower lip. That has to be about the dumbest explanation I've ever heard. Then again, I still don't even know who the headmaster is. I follow Jade's gaze, which has settled on a red-faced, mustached man sitting four seats down from Madam Lecter. He looks stern and a bit unhappy, but who knows? Maybe he's sentimental too?

Sentimental or not, when we return to our table, Leroy, Jade, and I agree that the whole thing seems fishier than a great big tub of fish guts. I mean, what are the odds that Headmaster Cunningham decided he missed his family *on the exact same day* I let it slip that I could talk to the painting?

Not only that, but Madam Booth essentially confirmed that there's no portrait repair shop in the basement and that the pictures aren't commonly moved around the school. Which means that unless Headmaster Cunningham really is feeling homesick at an extraordinarily dubious time, Josephine's disappearance feels . . . personal.

Like she went missing *because of me*. Because of what she could tell me.

Which of course makes me want to find her all the more.

The mystery is never far from my mind all throughout the day, but it isn't until the middle of the night that my brain finally hatches a plan. A very simple, very straightforward, supremely brilliant plan to determine once and for all if Madam Lecter's guess was right.

And, as a major bonus, all I need to do is sneak out of my bed, break into the headmaster's office, and have a little look around.

What can go wrong?

16

The Headmaster's Office

I fling off my covers and slide from bed, thrilled to finally be doing something. Owing to the whole my-feet-never-touch-the-ground thing, Leroy doesn't hear my footsteps as I float to our door. This is good. Really good. Leroy might be one of my new best friends, but the goody-goody would 100 percent, no doubt about it, as sure as the sky is orange, try to talk me out of my plan.

Jade, on the other hand, would totally be up for an adventure. I'm sure of it. But considering I've got no clue which bedroom door is hers, I don't even know where to knock.

I'm on my own.

I glide into a hallway that's somehow blacker than pitch black. Figuring my super-sneaky, super-stealthy plan won't stay very super-sneaky or super-stealthy if I start crashing into walls and knocking stuff over, I stand perfectly still and wait for my eyes to adjust. As soon as I can see my hands in front of my face, I take off for one of the back stairwells. It isn't until I reach the first floor that I realize I have no idea where to go next. Is the headmaster's office to the left? Or to the right?

After a moment of indecision, it hits me. I can ask the paintings!

Only problem is, there isn't enough light for me to tell if any given picture frame surrounds a portrait of a person . . . or a painting of a beach or a bridge or a wombat. At least Leroy, Jade, and I walked down this hallway back when we went exploring after our first day of school. So I close my eyes and try to remember, remember, remember.

Mister Grumpy Man!

There was a picture of a grumpy man with his puppy somewhere around here. I squint into the darkness until I make out a promising outline on one of the canvases.

"Excuse me. Do you know where the headmaster's office is?"

There is just enough motion in the picture for me to know the man is shaking his head. Well, snot buckets. I'm 0 for 1.

I walk a little farther, trying to find the painting of the circus. A muffled elephant trumpet tells me I'm heading in the right direction. I follow the sound and repeat my question to the blob closest to the front, which I assume is the ringmaster. Thankfully, he turns out to be way more helpful than Mister Grumpy Man. He tells me to take a left at the end of the hall and keep going until I reach a Medusa statue.

This, I can do.

A few minutes later, I'm hovering in front of a closed door. It's loads too dark to read the nameplate, but my fingers can make out just enough letters on its embossed surface to confirm that I'm in the right place.

My arm reaches for the doorknob but freezes as doubts rush at me—in my mom's *Think before you act* voice, of course. I can't hear any noise coming from the other side of the thick wood, but what if the headmaster is still inside, finishing up on some last-minute work? Or what if his office is booby-trapped? Maybe the second the door opens, a bottle of reeking grandma perfume will be spritzed all over my face. Or a giant vat of Kevin's beloved brown mash will be dumped upon my head.

I consider Mom's advice for all of two seconds before brushing it aside. Risks or no risks, I'm not scurrying back to my room with my tail between my legs. I'm not leaving until I get some answers.

I twist the doorknob, the door inches open, and I wait...

No perfume sprays.

No "food" plummets.

I let out my breath and step inside the room.

A dying fire (a dying *purple* fire!) in the corner fireplace lights up the room just enough for me to make out a gigantic desk, a wall of bookshelves, and the bust of some presumedly very-important person bearing a long skinny nose and eyebrows like fuzzy caterpillars. The room smells like a mixture of smoke and pine trees.

Three pictures hang on the walls. The first is of a building I know I've seen in photos before. Westminster Abbey perhaps? Five tail-wagging Chihuahuas in miniature pink tutus dance around in the second. And the third is a portrait of a woman who looks *exactly* like Mustache Lady. Apart from the fact that she has no mustache.

I step closer to the third picture. "Josephine?"

The lady's brown eyes blink in surprise. Clearly nobody has ever spoken to her before.

"That is not Josephine."

I spin around and come face-to-face with the headmaster. His normally stern expression is sterner than usual. Even though ghosts don't technically have beating hearts, mine feels like it's going a million beats per second. "That woman was my mother."

Now that he says it, I can see the resemblance. Her face is rosy, like the headmaster's. They have the same deep crease between their eyes. And they both have arms that seem oddly large when compared to the rest of their bodies, like snowmen with logs for arms instead of branches.

But their expressions? *Those* are different. The headmaster's mother looks confused but kind; the headmaster looks like he'd love nothing more than to unravel the secret of what happens to a ghost (translation: me) if you toss it into a black hole.

"Do you care to tell me what you're doing in my office in the middle of the night, son?" the headmaster asks.

Nope. That's pretty much the very last thing I want to do.

As the silence stretches on and on and on like the song that never ends, the headmaster's face grows increasingly red.

I'd better say something. And fast.

I rack my brain for a story that could realistically explain why I'm standing where I'm standing, but like usual, my brain strikes out. Big-time.

I can only think up one excuse, and it's not a good one.

"I got lost looking for the bathroom?" I cringe at the way my words sound more like a question than an answer.

"If I remember correctly, there are five fully functioning bathrooms on the third floor and four on the second. And yet your search led you all the way down two flights of stairs. How odd." The headmaster throws a log onto the fire and waits for me to say something.

Once again, the silence drags on.

And on.

And on.

If I could sweat, I'd be a waterfall.

Finally, the deafening silence becomes too much.

"I sleepwalk a lot, sir. I probably sleepwalked down the stairs."

I hardly keep from slapping my own forehead. I don't even know if ghosts sleep, so why would they sleepwalk?

Instead of yelling or stomping his feet or throwing me into a black hole, the headmaster tilts his head. His eyes drill into mine like a jackhammer drilling into a jar of strawberry jelly. "You're Finn Winters, aren't you?"

I want to say no—to tell him my name is Kevin or Rebecca or Bugs Bunny—but I'm pretty sure the headmaster won't fall for that. I nod.

Headmaster Cunningham leans closer. He smells *exactly* like my grandpa. Memories of trips to Dodger Stadium and stargazing on the lido deck threaten to undo any semblance of composure I have left. I quickly slam the door on these thoughts, forcing myself to focus on the here and now.

"So, you are the one all the teachers are talking about. You have them quite stirred up, Master Winters."

"I do?" Apart from Mister Zilla and Mister Gruber's hushed conversation yesterday, I haven't noticed anything odd. Then again, I'm not exactly the king of observational skills. Once my mom cut off ten inches of hair to donate to Locks of Love, and I didn't notice for a week.

"You do. They all want to know if you can really talk to the portraits like you claimed you could. I've asked them to give you time, to let you settle in at Phantom Academy for a bit before interrogating you about it. But since you're standing here in front of me now, is it true?"

Fart.

FArt.

FARt.

FART.

FART!

What am I supposed to say now? A minute ago, Headmaster Cunningham *heard* me ask his mom if she was Josephine, so he's likely already guessed the answer. If I come clean about everything and explain what I'm looking for, maybe, just maybe, he'll be on my side. Maybe he'll even help me find Mustache Lady.

But what if the headmaster is the one who moved the painting in the first place? What if *he's* the one who doesn't want me talking to her? Maybe he's afraid she'll tell me some colossal family secret that will destroy the family name forever. Like the Cunninghams were responsible for starting World War I. Or they were the ones to kill the very last dodo bird.

What if instead of helping me, Headmaster Cunningham takes after his great-grandpa—Sir Arthur George Cunningham III? What if he decides to silence me, just like how I'm beginning to suspect Sir Arthur silenced his sister?

Can I risk it?

After a moment of indecision, I decide the answer is no. I *can't* risk it. I'll tell the headmaster I lied. That I love making up stories because I crave attention.

PHANTOM ACADEMY

I open my mouth, but before I can say a single word, a *crash* saves the day.

A crash coming from out in the hallway.

Just outside the headmaster's office.

17

Medusa Meets Her End

The headmaster and I whirl toward the door like a couple of twirling ballerinas. Then he rushes out of the office, with me at his heels.

The purple light spilling out into the hallway quickly reveals what happened: Someone knocked over the Medusa statue. Long fragments of snake hair are everywhere, spinning around and around like pinwheels. Medusa's body lies in a million pieces.

"Cook?" the headmaster yells as a flash of red disappears around a corner. "Come back!"

But the cook and his red hair are long gone. Vanishing just like yesterday.

The confusion on the headmaster's face matches my own. Why is the cook wandering through the deserted corridors in the middle of the night?

And could it have anything to do with Mustache Lady's disappearance?

As hard as it is, I force all thoughts of the cook out of my head. I need to make the most of this well-timed distraction. Hunching over, I hop from foot to foot, all while twisting my face into a pained grimace. "Umm . . . sir? I still need that bathroom. Can I please go now?"

The headmaster's eyebrows arch suspiciously, but eventually, he nods. "Come back if you ever want to talk, Finn. My door is always open, though I'd prefer you came during daytime hours."

I waddle down the hall to keep up the I-really-need-to-pee charade, but as soon as I'm out of the headmaster's sight, I'm off. Racing back to my bedroom and collapsing onto my bed. So far as I can tell, Leroy hasn't moved a muscle since I left the room ages ago. And he goes right on not moving a muscle until *finally* the wake-up bell rings.

As Jade, Leroy, and I make our way to Table Eight for

breakfast, I tell them all about my middle-of-the-night escapade. Not surprisingly, they both get upset. Leroy because of my careless rule breaking. Jade because I didn't invite her along.

"The cook sure is acting suspicious, though," Jade says after she finally forgives me for going solo—*and* after she gives me very, very clear directions on exactly where her bedroom is, so she doesn't miss out on another quest. "We'd better keep an eye on him."

"I agree." Even though I don't see the cook anywhere, the pile of moldy, orange, pancake-like things sitting on my plate confirms he's still around. He must not have gotten sacked in the middle of the night.

"I'm less worried about the cook than I am about Headmaster Cunningham saying you've got the teachers stirred up, Finn." Leroy stabs his pancakes like they'd just insulted his favorite book. "It makes me nervous. Plus, if they're all watching you, it will be harder for us to plan our escape."

"I'm sure he was exaggerating," I say, trying to reassure him. But as we go throughout the day, it turns out the headmaster was right.

Now that I'm paying attention, it's clear the teachers *are* acting weird.

Madam Booth looks at Rebecca; Leroy; the ceiling; the

chalkboard; the backs of her wrinkly, speckled, old-lady hands—basically anywhere but at me. It's as though she's afraid questions will start flying out of her mouth should we accidentally make eye contact.

Mister Gruber refuses to call on me when I raise my hand to ask about Phantom Academy's sewer system. Our history teacher has never much *liked* answering student questions, but this is a whole new level of avoidance, even for him. Perhaps he misunderstood Headmaster Cunningham's directive, and instead of avoiding asking *me* questions, he thinks he needs to avoid answering mine.

It isn't until BTBGYCB class that I finally come across an adult who doesn't treat me differently from my classmates. Having finished talking about the rules of ghosthood yesterday, today Madam Lecter declares we'll be starting a new unit. A unit that will give us an overview of all the things we can be and do after graduating from Phantom Academy.

We can become teachers or builders.

Authors or therapists.

Gardeners or cooks.

We can even become enforcers, the ghosts in charge of making sure all the other ghosts follow the rules.

"But why would a ghost *want* to work?" Rebecca asks.

"Is there ghost money to earn? Ghost yachts to buy? Ghost malls to go shopping in?"

Madam Lecter shakes her head. "No, there is no currency or commerce in the Spirit Realm like what you had in the Land of the Living."

"Then I don't get it. What's the point of working?" As Rebecca twirls a lock of blond hair around her pointer finger, I wonder if she's ever worked a day in her life. Did she have any chores at all? Like washing the dishes? Raking the lawn? Picking up dog poo?

"For all kinds of reasons, Rebecca. A job helps pass the time. It makes us feel like our existence matters. It's a way to give back. Don't you think you'll eventually grow bored if you spend all your time hanging out in movie theaters and concert halls and football stadiums?"

Ummm . . . no. That sounds amazing!

"As a teacher," Madam Lecter continues, "I get to help educate future ghosts and set them on the right path. I find my job very rewarding, though it doesn't come without sacrifice."

My classmates and I share a look.

Sacrifice?

Do ghost teachers get dangled over an ectoplasm-craving volcano every hundred years or so to appease some vicious Spirit Realm god? Or is she talking about a different kind of sacrifice?

Finally, Jade raises her hand and asks the question we're all thinking: "Sacrifice? What sacrifice?"

"Well, us teachers are always here, aren't we? With you. Other ghosts get to visit their families and watch their kids and grandkids grow up, but we're only permitted to leave campus one night a month. It's bad enough that my son's grown-up and I'll never again get to run my fingers through his hair like I did when he was little, or kiss away his boo-boos, or sing him to sleep, but this job makes it so that I'm not allowed to *see* him for weeks at a time."

Hearing Madam Lecter complain about only seeing her family once a month immediately accomplishes two things.

First, it unlocks an entirely new level of pessimism inside my brain. It means I can essentially cross the follow-the-teachers-around-at-night-until-one-of-them-leads-us-to-the-school's-top-secret-exit strategy off my list of ways to escape Phantom Academy. Given how rarely the teachers leave, I'd have more luck trying to get an A in writing class.

And second, it makes my nonexistent blood boil. Madam Lecter obviously doesn't realize how lucky she is.

I'd give *anything* to know I'd get to see my family once a month! Heck, I'd give anything just to see them one more time. To hear Madison's giggle once more. To smell my mom's citrusy shampoo once more. To see my dad smiling one of his signature crooked smiles once more.

I'm still low-key fuming about Madam Lecter's woe-is-me nonsense when BTBGYCB class ends and we float down the two flights of stairs to Room B8. Clearly I'm not the only one in a mood either, because the room feels less like the Land of the Living and more like a morgue.

Everybody is silent.

Everybody, that is, except Mister Zilla.

He glides over to Jade and yells at her to "Focus!"

He sidles up to Rebecca and barks at her to "Stop wasting time admiring your fingernails!"

He slithers over to Kevin and demands that he "Stop daydreaming about food!"

He even tells Leroy—whose face is so scrunched in concentration that he looks like a raison—to "Concentrate!"

But when I wander over to the window and spend ten whole minutes gazing out at the Land of the Living's bright blue sky, all he does is shoot malevolent looks my way from the far side of the room. It's as though the headmaster's edict to leave me alone has left Mister Zilla believing his head might explode if he comes within five feet of me.

"Are you both annoyed too?" I ask when I finally leave the window and join Leroy and Jade in the kitchen, where they've teamed up to turn on the faucet. Like normal, they've been thoroughly unsuccessful. "It's so frustrating to hear a teacher complain about only leaving once a month when we're looking at a five-year sentence."

"Yeah, it's got me missing my family extra hard right now. Even my hermana María, if you can believe it."

"I miss my sister, too," I say. It's kind of strange, actually. When I was alive, I spent most of my time trying to avoid Madison, who was endlessly begging me to do stuff with her. But now? I'd happily sit crisscross applesauce on the floor and play dolls with her for hours. I'd even join her on the couch for a *Bluey* marathon, so long as it was guaranteed that Judo wouldn't be making a cameo.

Leroy doesn't say anything, but as he chews away at his bottom lip, I know exactly what he's thinking about: brothers and Frisco RoughRiders baseball games and reams of regret.

"I wonder if everyone feels closer to their siblings after they die," I say at last. Maybe death makes us realize what's truly important—only at that point, it's too late.

Jade shakes her head. "Not everyone. Not Sir Arthur George Cunningham III."

My head jerks up. *Mustache Lady was Sir Arthur's sister!*

I've known that since the beginning, of course, but I hadn't really thought about it until now. Surely, he must know Mustache Lady better than anyone else.

"I need to talk to Sir Arthur's painting!" I whisper.

Not only will Sir Arthur likely know what happened to the real Josephine, but if I can somehow win him over to our side, he might be able to help us puzzle out where her portrait disappeared to. And maybe, just maybe, he'll know why someone would *resort to thievery* just to keep me from talking to her.

For the rest of class, Jade, Leroy, and I debate the details. Mister Zilla is clearly beyond annoyed by our now-constant chatter, but thanks to the protective bubble Headmaster Cunningham put around me, he does nothing but glare.

"We should go after lights out," Jade argues for the umpteenth time. "We'll be far less likely to be seen or overheard."

"I am not breaking any rules," Leroy insists, his arms crossed over his chest.

Jade and I try to wear him down, but eventually, Leroy's

unwavering dedication to the goody-two-shoes way wears us down instead.

Finally, it's settled. Two hours after dinner, when most ghosts will hopefully be in their bedrooms, I'm having a little one-on-one chat with Mustache Lady's big brother.

18

Sir Arthur Gets MAD

"Remember the plan?" I ask when it's finally go time. "Leroy, you stand guard at the bottom of the stairs. Jade, you keep watch by me and Sir Arthur."

"Sounds good. We'll whistle if we see anyone coming, won't we, Leroy?"

A look of uncertainty creeps across Leroy's face. He purses his lips . . . then blows. He sounds like a toddler trying to make wind noises. He blows harder . . . and sounds like a toddler trying to make really loud wind noises.

"Darn it. I was hoping maybe I could whistle, now that I'm dead."

"It's okay," Jade says, holding up a hand to hide her smile. "You can clap instead."

Jade and Leroy take up their positions as I approach Sir Arthur George Cunningham III's portrait. The man doesn't notice me. He's too busy combing his mustache.

I clear my throat. "Hello, Sir Arthur," I say with as much politeness as I can muster for this man I've grown to hate. Somehow I've got to get him to like me.

Sir Arthur says nothing.

"How is your day going?" I ask.

Sir Arthur says nothing.

"The sky's extra orange today, isn't it?"

Again, Sir Arthur says nothing, although this time I can't blame him. It's not like he can wander over to a window and look outside anytime he wants. How would he know about the weather?

Not wanting to say anything even more stupid, I force myself to stop and think. Mom always says the best way to get a person talking is to give them a compliment. I might as well give her strategy a shot.

"Your mustache is looking particularly bushy today, sir."

Sir Arthur turns to face me, and my jaw almost hits the floor. Mom's strategy actually works?!

"Are you speaking to me?" Sir Arthur asks.

"Uh-huh."

Sir Arthur carefully sets down his comb, which has a silver handle decorated with tiny pearls. As his eyes narrow, I'm struck by how similar *and* how different they are from his sister's eyes. And from *my* mom's eyes. They might all be the same shade of brown and have the same slightly upturned shape, but his are missing all the warmth and sparkle.

"Your sister could talk to paintings too, couldn't she?"

"She said she could, but I never believed her." He looks like he isn't sure he believes me either, even though we're in the middle of a person-to-painting conversation right now. "Maybe I should have."

I nod, and for the briefest of seconds, an emotion flickers across his face. Sadness perhaps?

This is all it takes for my hopes to soar. Maybe he feels guilty over how he treated Josephine all those years ago. Maybe he'll want to unburden himself by spilling his guts to me, right here, right now.

"What happened to your sister, if you don't mind me asking?" I keep my voice nice and gentle, exactly like my mom does whenever she wants me to part with some precious piece of information I desperately want to keep hidden. Like *Why are your brand-new shoes covered in red paint?* Or *How did your math test go?* Or *Is there a reason all of Madison's dolls are missing their hair?*

I'm expecting Sir Arthur's face to collapse in sorrow or shame, but nope. It fills with rage instead.

"What happened to my sister? She betrayed me, that's what happened!" A giant glob of saliva flies out of his mouth, soars right through the painting, and squelches onto the floor a mere inch from my hovering sneakers. "My own sister went behind my back, and she got *exactly* what she deserved."

I stumble backward as Sir Arthur's fury washes over me. Even though he's trapped inside his frame, the man—and his anger—are terrifying.

"How did she betray you?" I ask once I find my voice again. "And what did she get?"

But Sir Arthur's stop-sign red face is clammed up tight.

I decide to switch gears and try asking him about the brown, streaking thing instead. Partly just to get him talking again and partly because I really, really want to know what that thing was. Before I can say anything, though, a shrill whistle sounds from my left, nearly making me jump out of my shoes.

It takes a second for my brain to realize it's Jade, signaling that someone is coming.

I know I should be disappointed that I can't keep peppering Sir Arthur with questions, but I'm not. A part of me even thanks my Lucky Charms that I have an excuse to get far, far away from Sir Arthur George Cunningham III and the storm of malice now swirling around his portrait. Sure as sure, *he* was the one who turned the entire ghost world against his sister.

I calmly—or as calmly as I can, considering Sir Arthur's got me shaking like a Shih Tzu in a thunderstorm—walk past the student who caused Jade to whistle. Her face follows me curiously, and I vaguely wonder how much she'd seen and heard.

As soon as Leroy, Jade, and I are fully out of the girl's sight, we race up the stairs and fall onto my bed.

"What happened back there?" Jade asks. "You looked terrified."

I fill them in on the last ten minutes and expect Jade and Leroy to be disappointed by my utter lack of success. Instead, Leroy becomes strangely animated. "You said Sir Arthur accused Josephine of going behind his back? You're sure those were his exact words?"

I reluctantly think through my conversation with the Mustached Monster again. "Yup, I'm positive. He said Josephine betrayed him by going behind his back. But that's normal sister stuff, isn't it? Madison, the little backstabber, was constantly tattling to Mom about everything I did."

Leroy's right leg starts bouncing—up and down, up and down, up and down—and the room fills with the *zwip, zwip, zwip* of his corduroy pants rubbing together. "I suspect it means more than that. Think about it . . . What is the main thing Sir Arthur and Josephine disagreed about?"

Oh gosh. What did brothers and sisters fight about in the early eighteenth century? Who won at marbles? Who got first dibs on the rocking horse? Who had the itchiest clothes?

But then it hits me, and I almost fall off the bed. "They disagreed about whether to let students into the Land of the Living. Do you think Josephine went behind Sir Arthur's back and created another thinning of the veil? Here? In the school?"

Leroy grins, and my whole body tingles with excitement.

"You mean . . . she and her portrait might know exactly how we can escape from Phantom Academy?" Jade's voice is hardly louder than a whisper. "They might help us break out of Alcatraz?"

"I don't really know, of course, but it makes sense, doesn't it?" Leroy's words hang in the air for one one-thousand,

two one-thousand,

three one-thousand,

before the room erupts into a maelstrom of squealing and laughing and blobfishy high-fiving. Even Leroy lets loose with a whoop or two.

Finally, it all makes sense. Mustache Lady didn't want me to leave the school because she didn't like my freckles or because she wanted me to find something hidden on the school grounds; she probably wanted me to go use her super-secret door and get out of the Spirit Realm entirely. That way she'd finally have the kind of school she'd always wanted. A school where the students were free to visit the Land of the Living.

Which means . . . finding her portrait is my ticket home. My ticket back to my family.

"I bet anything that Josephine's painting was taken so she couldn't tell me about the hidden exit. But who did it? And why?"

"We need a suspect list!" Leroy declares as he grabs a notebook and pen off his desk. A few minutes later, our list is complete:

CHIEF SUSPECTS

1. The cook. He's shown up twice in odd places and always seems to be running away.
2. Mister Gruber. He's clearly against kids entering the Land of the Living, and he keeps telling Finn not to trust Josephine.
3. The headmaster. He probably knows more about Sir Arthur, Josephine, and Phantom Academy than anyone else in the school. Therefore, it's quite plausible that he'd know about any secret exits.
4. Mister Zilla. Because Josephine seemed afraid of him ... and—as Finn says—"he's rotten enough."

"Okay, so what do we do now?" Jade asks.

I glance over at the stack of Hardy Boys books on Leroy's desk. I may not be the mystery lover that Leroy is, but my grandma has forced me to watch enough episodes of *Monk* with her that even I know where we should start. "Simple. We go back to the scene of the crime and look for clues!"

19

Suspect Number One

Without wasting a second, we rush outside Leroy's and my room. The cat puffs away on his pipe as we look around. But as it turns out, looking for clues is hard to do when all one's suspects are ghosts. Not only do ghosts not leave footprints (thanks to the whole feet-don't-touch-the-ground thing), but we also don't shed hair. Which, come to think of it, is rather fortunate. Otherwise, we'd all wind up looking like Mr. Potato Head dolls before too long.

"Wait! Is this a crumb?" Jade asks. She's on her hands and knees, probing the groves in the stone floor for anything unusual. She picks up a brown speck and holds it up to the candle sconce. "Maybe it fell off the cook's clothing when he was switching out the pictures?"

Leroy takes the tiny object from Jade and scrutinizes the thing from every angle. "Too bad we don't have a microscope," he grumbles.

"Even if it is a crumb, we already know the cook was up here that day. I'm not sure this adds much." I can't quite keep the frustration from my voice. We *need* to solve this mystery. Not only could it be the key to seeing my family again, but Josephine cofounded this school. Her picture should be at the top of the main stairwell next to Sir Arthur's, not hidden down some third-floor hallway, and *certainly* not missing.

I meander around, looking for more clues, and eventually find myself floating in front of the man on the unicycle. The guy is *still* biking; how he isn't exhausted is beyond me.

"Do you remember me from a couple of days ago?" I ask. He nods once. "Remember how I asked you about a missing painting? Can you tell me anything about that day? Anything at all?"

Unicycle Man shakes his head. Like last time, his gaze keeps shifting behind me. It's as though he thinks he'll get in major trouble if he's caught talking to me. Or maybe he's afraid it will get *me* in major trouble if we're caught talking?

"Ask him if he's seen the cook around," Jade whispers as she comes up behind me.

I relay the question, and, after a moment of indecision, Unicycle Man gives me a curt nod.

"Have you seen the cook carrying a picture?"

Unicycle Man shakes his head.

"So you haven't seen the cook holding a picture, but he's been around. Is he around a lot? Like more than a few times?"

A nod.

I try to ask more questions, but Unicycle Man has had enough.

"It *is* the cook!" Jade declares when I fill her and Leroy in on the conversation. "It has to be."

"But he has no motive," Leroy says. "Obviously we don't know the cook all too well, but still. What would he gain by moving it?"

"You already said it: We don't know the cook," Jade argues. "Maybe he uses the exit to sneak out of the school every night for cooking lessons, because *surely* his job's in jeopardy if he doesn't improve soon. Or maybe he has this whole other side to him, like how Bruce Wayne is also Batman or how Clark Kent is also Superman, only the cook's other side is as an art thief or something."

In the end, we decree that a stakeout is in order. It's almost lights out now, so we decide that tomorrow, after dinner, the three of us will become the cook's shadow. We will follow him and follow him and follow him until we either discover his secret . . . or die again, this time out of boredom.

All through dinner the next night, I watch the long hand of the clock *tick, tick, tick* off the minutes. Kevin is the only one at our table who seems perfectly content as he polishes off four bowls of the neon pink stew that constitutes tonight's dinner. Somehow the pink sludge manages to be chunky and gelatinous, all at the same time.

"Finally!" Jade exclaims when the bell rings and the room empties out. "I swear that was the longest hour of my afterlife."

I laugh and point to the table closest to the kitchen. "I'm thinking we should hide under there."

"Works for me." Jade lifts the tablecloth, and the three of us slip underneath. The space is dark, cramped, and very smelly, thanks to the five untouched bowls of stew sitting directly above us.

I'm starting to think I picked the wrong hiding place when the cook's voice begins drifting out from the kitchen. It's all grumbles and moans and complaints about how nobody ever touches his food. How he puts all this work into the meals and most of it ends up in the trash. How that skinny kid in the Buzz Lightyear pajamas is the only one who appreciates the good food he's given.

I'm sorely tempted to pop out and suggest he try cracking open one of the cookbooks Jade and I had spotted in the kitchen, but for once I rein in the impulse.

After what feels like three lifetimes, the cook has cleared off the last table, scrubbed the last dish, and has astonishingly run out of things to complain about. He leaves the cafeteria.

And we follow.

He goes down one hallway. Up a flight of stairs. Down another hallway. Down another flight of stairs. Weaving up and down, back and forth, like he's seriously determined not to be followed.

Jade shoots me an excited look, and I shoot one back. I've never *actually* thought the cook was the one who moved the painting, yet here he is. Acting all funny.

Eventually, the cook turns into a tiny, out-of-the-way hallway on the second floor and pulls out a key.

"What is he doing?" Jade hisses. "His room is on the first floor. I'm sure of it."

We watch from around the corner as the cook unlocks the door and squats. Half his body is in the room. Half is still out in the hall.

"How's my good boy?" The cook's voice no longer oozes grumpiness. Instead, it's light and bubbly. Like how my mom's voice gets when she's talking to a baby. "Did you miss me?"

I take a tentative step into the hallway, hoping to catch a glimpse of whomever the cook is talking to, but my foot freezes mid-step when a chocolate-colored blur erupts from the room. The cook is sent flying backward as a blanket of brown encases him. Not even his bright red hair escapes the attack.

Leroy, Jade, and I jump back and share a panicked look.

What do we do?

Charge in and attempt a rescue?

Run for our lives before the brown blur polishes off its first victim and looks for a second?

Call for help? Although how would one even report a ghost murder anyway? Does the Spirit Realm have its own ghostly version of 911?

Before we can make up our minds, the air fills with laughter. The *cook's* laughter.

He's alive!

(Or at least not further dead.)

I leave a trembling Leroy and Jade behind as I tiptoe into the hallway to investigate. At first I can't make heads or tails of the chaos in front of me, but then I figure it out. A massive brown dog—a kinda, sorta, not-really-see-through, massive brown dog—is lying on top of the cook. His wagging tail *flawps* against the cook's leg as he covers him in slobbery dog kisses.

"It's safe," I call back to my friends.

At my words, the cook bolts upright. His back ramrod straight. His jaw clenched. His laughter gone.

Jade rounds the corner and—upon seeing the dog—lets out a delighted squeal that reaches a pitch I don't think even Madison can achieve. It's a rather impressive accomplishment, actually, but the cook doesn't look impressed at all. Instead, he looks equal parts furious and scared.

"Hush! Please! Be quiet!"

His head swivels back and forth, watching, no doubt, to see if Jade's outburst will bring a stampede of curious ghosts streaming our way. When it finally becomes clear that nobody else is coming, the cook relaxes. "Sorry for jumping down your throats, but pets are strictly forbidden in Phantom Academy."

"Don't worry, we won't tell anyone. Will we, guys?" Jade says.

"Of course not, I love dogs!" I used to beg for one all the time, but my dad was allergic.

"Do all animals turn into ghosts?" Leroy asks, not really answering Jade's question. "Could Nibbles be a ghost?"

"Nibbles?" Jade snorts. "You named your dog *Nibbles?*"

"Nibbles wasn't a dog. He was a hamster. The best hamster in the world, if you want to know the truth. He died when I was five."

"The best in the world, huh?" Jade laughs as she crouches down and holds out her hand. The ghost dog pads over and sniffs her fingers. She must pass muster because the dog's tail somehow starts wagging even harder, and soon his entire ghostly butt is wagging too. Jade quickly gives up any semblance of restraint as she smothers him in hugs and smooches and back scratches. When the dog doesn't bite off any of Jade's fingers, I collapse next to her and join in the fun. Even Leroy gives the dog a quick pat on the head.

The cook watches us for a minute before turning to Leroy. "I'm sorry, kid, but I don't think you'll find Nibbles here." Considering the cook looks like he's no more than a year or two older than us, it's a bit unnerving hearing him call Leroy a kid. "As with people, most animals do not become ghosts. Most go the other way."

Leroy's face collapses, but Jade isn't relinquishing her hope so easily. "How do I get *my* hands on a dog?"

"After you graduate, explore the Spirit Realm until you find one. That's how I got Bucky here. But consider yourself warned: ghost animals are not allowed in the Land of the Living, and ghost humans are not allowed to remain in the Spirit Realm for very long unless they have an approved reason. That's why I took the position here as a cook, even though the job is terrible. Bucky is worth it though, aren't you, boy."

"But that makes no sense. You said dogs aren't allowed in Phantom Academy, either." Leave it to Leroy to debate the rules.

"That's true, I guess, but it's totally different. If we're caught here, I'll simply take Bucky somewhere else. I'll find another job in the Spirit Realm. If he's caught in the Land of the Living, though, he'll be moved on." The cook scratches Bucky under his chin. "But don't you worry, boy. I'll never let that happen. You and me, we'll be together forever."

Once Jade, Leroy, and I get our fill of dog breath and dog slobber, we head back to our rooms, satisfied that we've discovered the truth behind why the cook (whose name is apparently David) was sneaking around. Not only did he tell us that he alters his route to Bucky's room with every visit, but he and Bucky often walk the corridors after lights out. It was Bucky, the furry little saint, who knocked over the Medusa statue while I was in the headmaster's office. David even admitted to periodically sneaking Bucky into the kitchen and letting him out the back door to run around in the garden, meaning we solved the mystery of the ominous, brown, streaking thing too.

Being able to cross Suspect Number One off our list definitely feels good. We're making progress.

Only three more suspects to go.

20

Cats and Mustache Envy

When Leroy and I step out of our bedroom the next morning, Jade is already there. Waiting for us once again.

"So? What do we do next to figure things out?" Neither of us needs to ask what Jade means by "things." "Have either of you come up with a plan?"

Leroy's gaze drops to his shoes, but thankfully I've had a semi-successful night of brainstorming. "I actually did come up with a way to test Mister Gruber. I'm not sure if it will work, and it will almost certainly make me look ridiculous, but I'm going to give it a try anyway."

"You don't need a 'plan' to make yourself look ridiculous, Finn," Jade teases. "You accomplish that simply by being you."

I give her a playful shove. "*I* look ridiculous? At least I'm not walking around with twigs sticking out of my hair."

Leroy cracks up as Jade's face twists in indignation. "Whoa, that was a pretty low blow there, bud. But I'll forgive you, just this once, because I really do want to hear your plan. Now spill it."

We float in silence for a minute as I think through things again. "You know what, the plan might work better if you two aren't in on it. That way your reactions will be genuine."

This answer is clearly *not* okay with Jade. All through breakfast, through reading class, through writing class, she begs me to let her in on the secret—even going so far as to slip me a note saying, "TELL ME RIGHT NOW OR I'LL NEVER SPEAK 2 U AGAIN!"—but I remain stubbornly quiet.

By the time Mister Gruber enters the room at exactly 11:00 a.m., Jade is practically jumping out of her seat. Our history teacher starts off with his customary (and completely unnecessary) "Settle down, class!" and then he's off. Lecturing.

"As you all know, we finished our unit on Phantom Academy yesterday. So today, we'll be starting our unit on the First Ghost War."

I can't help but sit up straighter in my seat. I mean, sure, I don't want to learn about *three hundred* ghost wars, but learning about a few of them sounds super interesting, right?

And things really do start out great. Mister Gruber explains how about three hundred thousand years ago, two bands of ghosts were locked in a bitter dispute. The issue? What to do with the ghost saber-toothed tigers and ghost giant sloths and ghost woolly mammoths that occasionally ended up in the Spirit Realm.

Should they be allowed to stay? Or be forced to move on?

Despite this promising beginning, though, it soon becomes clear that ghost wars are 100 percent *not* as cool as they sound. Ghosts cannot have their heads lopped off by hand axes. Or their bodies fatally impaled by spears. Or their brains turned to mush by giant rocks to the head. Which means that all ghost wars to date have winded up being more like a cross between a colossal shouting match and a cafeteria food fight.

Not that this fact dampers Mister Gruber's enthusiasm in any way. He's eagerly explaining the "fighting" tactics utilized by one of his favorite ghost generals when I remember my plan. And raise my hand.

At first it seems like Headmaster Cunningham's mandate might still have Mister Gruber too afraid to call on me, but finally he nods. "Yes, Finn? You have a question about General Mills?"

"No, sir. I miss my cat."

Rebecca snorts. Leroy gasps. And Mister Gruber's forehead creases until he looks like a bulldog. "I'm sorry you miss your cat, but maybe that's something you should discuss later. *With your friends.*"

"Okay, yeah, that's probably a good idea, but Mister Gruber? I don't think that will be enough. I miss Pumpkin too much. She was an orange tabby cat with kiwi-green eyes. Maybe if I can see a picture of a cat that looks exactly like her, I'll be able to focus better on your thrilling lessons from now on. You know this school better than I do; is there a picture of a cat like that on any of the walls?"

Mister Gruber blinks once. Twice. Three times. He clearly can't believe he's being asked about *cats* while in the middle of one of his riveting lectures.

"I think there is a cat like that on the third floor," Kevin chimes in. "In one of the side hallways."

"Thank you, Kevin," I say, even as I keep my attention

fixated on our teacher. I scan his bulldoged-up face for any sign of guilt or remorse or worry, but I don't see any of these emotions. I only see confusion. And loads of irritation.

"Well, it appears there is a cat like that on the third floor," Mister Gruber says. "And with that annoying interruption over with, I'm returning to my lesson."

Jade can't stop cackling as we head back to the cafeteria after class. "You definitely succeeded in making yourself look foolish, Finn. I thought Rebecca was going to bust a gut from laughing so hard. I don't understand how you thought talking about a cat would help us, but at least it was entertaining."

"Actually," Leroy says slowly, "I think Finn was rather brilliant. If Mister Gruber were the one to put the cat picture there, surely he'd have reacted in some way, especially after Kevin mentioned seeing it. Only a master criminal could have avoided giving anything away after being blindsided like that."

"Maybe Mister Gruber *is* a master criminal," Jade retorts. "Or . . . maybe Finn is sort of brilliant after all. The doofus."

I barely resist the urge to air-skip the rest of the way to lunch. Rebecca and Kevin might still be looking at me like a dog ate my sanity, but who cares? I'm pretty sure we've ruled out Suspect Number Two!

"Say, Finn, are you planning to tell Mister Zilla you miss your cat too?" Jade asks.

My throat squeezes at that thought. "Not in a million years. I still have no idea how to rule him out. Or the headmaster. Do either of you have any ideas?"

Jade gives me a quick no, but Leroy looks thoughtful. "Motive," he finally says. "It all comes back to motive. If we can determine who gained the most by taking the painting, we should be able to figure out whodunit."

Jade pushes absentmindedly at her glasses. "That *sounds* good, Leroy, but we aren't positive why the painting was taken in the first place. So how do we figure out who has the most to gain from it being gone?"

"Jade is right," I say. "We're pretty sure the painting was taken because Josephine knows a secret way out of the school, but we don't know that for sure. Maybe, I don't know, maybe Mister Morte moved the painting because he was jealous of her mustache or something." After all, our Intro to Electives teacher—aka Mister Q-tip—has fuzzy white hair cocooning the top of his head and billowing out of his nose and ears, but his face itself? It's as hairless as a naked mole rat.

"Her mustache is pretty remarkable. And not many

women would have the guts to flaunt it either. Most would have shaved it off. Or waxed." Even as she shudders at the thought of waxing, Jade's admiration for the woman is palpable.

I've never cared much for mustaches myself, but there's no doubt that history is full of famous bushy upper lips. There's Albert Einstein's walrus mustache. Frida Kahlo's daring mustache-unibrow duo. And speaking of duos, who can forget Captain Jack Sparrow and his mustache-goatee combo? Certainly not me, being that my mom has made me watch the first few Pirates of the Caribbean movies like a thousand times each. (All because she thinks Will Turner is "dreamy.")

Not surprisingly, when I sit down in Intro to Electives class three hours later and am face-to-face with Mister Morte's naked-mole-rat face, my previous mustache musings come back at me like a boomerang.

As Mister Q-tip starts describing the classical music course we can sign up for next term if we so desire (which gets a great big "No, thank you!" from me), I raise my hand.

"Yes, Finn?" Mister Q-tip sounds überexcited. Probably because the poor ghost doesn't get many questions; his boring-as-boring-can-be lectures tend to put students into comas instead.

"What is your opinion on mustaches, sir? Do you like them?"

Mister Morte stares at me blankly for a full five seconds before he says anything. "Do I like what?"

"Mustaches," I repeat as Rebecca shakes her head and starts muttering to herself. While I can't make out most of what she says, I'm pretty sure I hear the words "ridiculous" and "juvenile" mixed among the rest. "You know, lip whiskers. Do you like them?"

"Not really. I'm more of a muttonchops guy."

Rebecca is still muttering to herself ("childish," "weird," "bunch of oddballs") as Mister Morte gets back to his dreary portrayal of some eminent seventeenth-century Baroque composer.

But Rebecca can laugh at me all she wants; I might seem childish and odd and juvenile, but I also just ruled out Mister Morte's monstrous mustache envy as a motive.

21

The Stairwell

Considering how quickly we ruled out the cook and Mister Gruber (and Mister Q-tip) as suspects in the Mustache Lady portrait snatching, I'm feeling high as a kite as Leroy, Jade, and I leave Intro to Electives class. We're getting so close!

By dinner tomorrow, we'll probably have the culprit in hand and then BOOM. We'll be off. Visiting our families.

My excitement over finding a way home is nearing Christmas-morning level, so clearly, I need to rein things in a bit. My heart is dreaming of a grand reunion that my brain knows can never happen. One where I get to feel

Mom's arms wrap me up in a cocoon-like hug while Dad claps me on the back. Where Madison squeals at the sight of me and begs nonstop until I agree to give her a piggyback ride all around our tiny living room. Where Grandpa speeds over to our house with a giant tub of chocolate chip cookie dough ice cream (my favorite!), so we can have an ice cream party under the stars.

Deep down I know the reality will be way different. My family won't be able to see me. Won't be able to hear me. Won't even know I'm there. But I want to go anyway.

More than anything.

Although now that I think about it, I've been so focused on the *leaving* part, I somehow haven't thought much about what comes next. "After we find a way out of here, do you two think you'll come back? Or will you stay with your families?" I ask.

"I'm definitely coming back." Leroy's response is immediate, like he's thought this all through already.

Which, knowing Leroy, he probably has.

"I like all our classes, and I like being with both of you. I didn't really have any friends at my old school, so this is nice. Not that I don't wish I were still alive, because I do, but being dead, here, with you both, it isn't so bad."

The thought of Leroy not having friends makes my

heart ache. Sure, he's a bookworm and a brownnoser and his rule following can get *majorly* annoying at times, but he's also about the nicest person I know. And the smartest. My heart aches even more—this time with guilt—when I realize that *I* probably wouldn't have been friends with him either. Living me was kinda stupid like that.

While my heart goes through its roller coaster of emotions, Jade slowly sorts out her own answer to my question. Her eyes fixate on a spot of nothingness across the room as she pulls a Rebecca and twirls a clump of rainbow hair around and around her pointer finger.

"Me too," she says finally. Her tone decisive. "Even though I probably spent more time hanging out with insects than I did with people back when I was alive, I still need *someone* to talk to. And I suppose you two weirdos will have to do."

"Wow, thanks a lot, Jade," I say with a laugh. "But I'll be back too." I'll never forget the time I was grounded for using Sharpies to draw some pretty awesome clown features on Madison's face. I almost died of boredom after two days of being stuck at home.

But as it turns out, leavings and comings and grand reunions are not something Leroy, Jade, and I need to worry about. At least not yet. Because our investigation? It doesn't just hit a wall. It smashes into one.

None of us can think up an ingenious way to rule out the headmaster or Mister Zilla as suspects, so we wind up spending every second of free time wandering around the school. Hoping against hope that we'll magically stumble upon Josephine's portrait.

Or the highly sought-after thinning in the veil.

Or even just the teensiest of clues to get us back on the chase.

Fast-forward a couple of weeks, and we've drifted through every hallway, studied every picture, opened every unlocked door.

We now know that the school has seventeen bathrooms, twelve statues (which would have been thirteen, had Medusa survived), three pianos, and five grandfather clocks, only two of which actually work. There is an entire wing on the second floor that's utterly devoid of furniture and a tiny, hidden-away room in the basement that has three disco balls dangling from the ceiling.

I've tried (unsuccessfully) to interrogate the Unicycle King again, and I've tried (equally unsuccessfully) to rekindle my conversation with Sir Arthur George Cunningham III. I've even started asking random pictures if they know of any secret exits out of the school.

But everywhere we turn, there's another dead end.

After yet another frustrating hour of fruitless wandering, Jade gives one of the broken grandfather clocks a good kick before sagging to the ground. We're in an abandoned classroom on the third floor, surrounded by nothing but busted bedroom furniture, yellowing blankets, and a handful of pillows missing half their stuffing. "I'm starting to forget things," she says in response to my bemused expression.

"Forget things? You mean you're getting dementia?" Leroy asks. "My grandpappy had dementia. I wonder—"

"It's not dementia," Jade says, cutting Leroy off before he can propose an outing to the library to research ghost memory disorders or something. "I'm starting to forget my life. My old life. Like what my tía's perfume smelled like and what my abuela's empanadas tasted like." Her voice cracks. "If we don't get out of here soon, I'm afraid it will all be gone."

I might not have been at Phantom Academy as long as Jade, but I can still understand what she's saying. My life from the Land of the Living is starting to get a bit fuzzy too. Before I died, I had to listen to my dad sing in the shower every single morning. I thought for sure his painfully off-key high notes and horridly croaky low ones would be seared into my memory bank forever. And yet there they go. Getting all hazy.

Instead of being a relief, the thought of permanently forgetting all those horrendous sounds is devastating. I collapse next to Jade.

Leroy follows soon after. "My nana used to say 'Good night, lil' Roy-Roy' every night before she headed off to bed. I know I'll always remember *what* she said, but it's getting harder to remember *how* she said it."

Before long, an Eeyore-level depression permeates the room, wriggling into my bones and weighing me down. The fact that I'm still hovering an inch above the ground must be some kind of miracle, because I feel like I've gained a thousand pounds.

"In a way, all this forgetting is sort of like dying again," Leroy says. "It's as though we're losing ourselves, bit by b—"

Whoosh! A pillow slams into Leroy's face, shocking him into silence. I take aim at Jade next. "I'm declaring this pity party to be officially over!"

"Oh, no you don't," Jade cries as she scrambles to her feet. She grabs a feather pillow and wallops me in the back of the head. Leroy grabs a frilly, pink throw pillow and joins the fight.

Ten minutes later, the classroom floor is littered with

pillow guts, my side hurts (as much as a ghost's side *can* hurt) from laughing so hard, and the grandfather clock—which may or may not have gotten knocked to the ground by Jade's butt as she attempted to avoid one of my deadly pillow assaults—has reached a whole new level of broken.

By the time we shuffle back into the hallway, I feel almost back to my normal self.

"Guys, check that out!" Leroy gestures toward the tall, rectangular painting mounted on the wall in front of us. The canvas is covered in jagged, snowcapped mountains illuminated by a blue moon. The span of hallway right in front of it feels like a walk-in freezer, thanks to the wind that's whistling and howling down the mountain pass. "See how low it is?"

I blink in surprise. How have we not noticed this before? The painting extends so far down, it almost touches the ground!

Bracing myself against the biting temps, I slide in closer. Jade beats me there, though, and gives the frame a tug. The whole thing hinges open, just like a door! Peeking inside, we find a narrow stone staircase spiraling down, down, down until it's eventually swallowed by shadows.

I let out a cheer as Jade does an awkward little happy dance next to me.

The hunt for our next clue is back on track!

22

Toy Soldiers and Wooden Horses

"Let's check it out!" I crouch down to avoid bonking my head on the low ceiling and am about ten steps down the staircase before I realize I can't hear Leroy or Jade behind me. I spin around and discover they're still up top. Exactly where I left them.

"Don't you think we should get some light first?" Jade's amused voice echoes eerily around my head.

Now that she mentions it, the stairwell *is* a bit dark. Not as black as Rebecca's heart or anything, but close.

I sheepishly climb back up the rough-hewn steps, and a few minutes later, we're back in action. This time with an oil lantern, filched from a nearby classroom, gripped tightly in Leroy's hand.

"Hidden stairs adventure, take two," I say as I begin the descent again. This time, Jade follows, but not Leroy. He still lingers up top.

"Is the door stuck?" I ask.

"No, it's not that. It's just . . . maybe I should wait here. What if something goes wrong and I need to get help?" Leroy's voice has gained a brand-new wobble. He definitely seemed afraid of heights when we were back in the library, and he's obviously *terrified* of fire . . . Could he be afraid of the dark too? Or tight spaces?

"Forget it, lil' Roy-Roy. You're coming with us. We might need your smarts." Jade tugs on Leroy's maroon T-shirt until he reluctantly steps through the gaping hole.

The painting swings shut behind him.

Even as a new level of darkness closes in around us, I push ahead, my hands trembling with excitement. I count twenty steps. Thirty. Fifty!

The lower we go, the more the air in the passageway starts feeling different from the rest of the school. Older. Staler. Forgotten. Forgotten by everything except the spiders, that is. Their webs are everywhere! I have to swing my arms wildly in front of me or risk ending up with a mouthful of yuck.

"Don't hurt them!" Jade cries after one of my more vigorous swipes. "I want to come back later and study them."

"You're welcome to lead the way if you want," I snap. "*You* can be the one with spiderwebs all over your face."

Jade falls silent, exactly as I knew she would. The girl's fearless about all kinds of things, but when it comes to recklessly leading the way into the unknown? That's ME territory.

"How many floors down do you think we've gone?" Jade asks, changing the subject.

"We must have gone down at least three by now, don't you think, Leroy?"

Leroy's only reply is an unintelligible moan. His eyes never stop moving—up, down, left, right—as though he thinks a ghost will jump out at us at any moment.

We drop another ten or so steps before the stairwell dead-ends in a small chamber packed with wooden crates and boxes. Mountains of dust coat every surface while yellowish-purple fingers of mold creep up the walls. An archaeologist would undoubtedly have a field day excavating through all the layers of grime, but I can't help but feel somewhat disappointed. There's no way we'll find Mustache Lady's portrait down here. I bet nobody's stepped foot in this room for decades.

Instead of giving in to despair, I force myself to unslump my shoulders. Maybe we won't find Josephine down here, but who knows? Maybe we'll find something else. Something better. Like the thinning of the veil itself, hiding behind a wooden crate or something.

Jade and I each pick a box and set to work prying off their lids. Leroy, meanwhile, stands in the middle of the room, lantern held high above his head, quivering like Jell-O. When Jade tries to get him to put down the lantern and join the search, he shakes his head, refusing to let go of the light.

It takes a bunch of tugging and wrenching and grunting, but finally I get my first box open. And discover it's full of . . . toy soldiers?

My second box contains a couple dozen porcelain-faced dolls with royally creepy eyes.

And the third? A slew of marbles and a handful of colorful kites with long, moth-eaten tails.

"I'm just finding toys," Jade says from the other side of the room after she rips open a large crate to reveal a collection of small, wooden horses on wheels. "A bunch of super old-fashioned toys."

"Me too. I wonder why."

It takes Jade, Leroy, and I a few minutes to work out a

theory, but in the end, I'm pretty sure we get it right. When Phantom Academy was being built, Josephine Cunningham probably envisioned the school quite differently from what we've ended up with today. Sure, it would be a place of learning, but the ghostly students would also get to play with toys, visit the Land of the Living, fly kites. But when Josephine went AWOL a year after the school was built, the toys were likely packed away and hidden down here. After all, why would Sir Arthur want *happy* kids at his school?

Cracking the Mystery of the Locked-Away Toys must evaporate whatever is left of Leroy's fears, because he finally sets down the lantern and joins in as we open the last few crates. "Whoa, check this out." He waves us over as he pushes a box full of spinning tops across the floor, revealing a Bernese-mountain-dog-sized gap in the wall. "I wonder where this leads."

"Only one way to find out." I drop to my hands and knees and stick my head through the hole. I only make it a few inches before my skull smacks into something hard. Ignoring Leroy's pleas to be careful, I reach into the darkness. My fingers probe around, feeling this way and that as they eagerly try to work out what I'd smashed into. It doesn't take long for me to determine that it's wooden and it's heavy and it's only a few inches thick.

Kind of like a framed painting!

I grit my teeth and carefully slide the object to the right, millimeter by millimeter by millimeter. It isn't easy, but eventually the path is clear.

Without pausing to think, I crawl toward the opening again, accompanied by nothing but the tiniest amount of wavering light. As soon as my head is fully in the next room, I look around.

And scream! Because *a ghost* is staring back at me from the opposite wall!

For a heartbeat, it's the fact that IT'S A GHOST that really gets to me, because somehow I've forgotten that I'm a ghost as well. As soon as this initial irrational fear vacates my head, though, I'm struck with an even worse one: What if this ghost has been locked away down here for a supremely good reason?

What if he's evil? Nefarious? Unspeakably vile? And I've just freed him from his prison? What if he's now at liberty to do something monstrous, like destroy the Spirit Realm itself?

I really, *really* need to learn how to think before I act.

The air fills with Leroy and Jade's panicked voices.

"Are you okay?!"

"What happened?!"

"Should we get help?!"

But I ignore them. I need to stay focused. I squint through the darkness and am shocked to discover that the loathsome ghost isn't Mister Zilla's age or Madam Booth's age or even Headmaster Cunningham's age.

He's *my* age.

Is it possible he isn't a fiend at all, but a *student*?

Is this what happens to kids who talk back too much in reading and writing class? They get sentenced to an eternity of solitary confinement?

It's at this moment that I notice the kid looks every bit as scared and confused and curious as I feel. Not only that, but he's also, quite oddly, down on all fours like I am.

I raise my right hand in a nervous wave, and it's only when the boy simultaneously waves back that the pieces come together. The ghost that nearly scared the poo out of me . . . was me.

Or rather, my reflection.

I let out a relieved laugh, which only increases the confused panic coming from the toy room behind me. After wiggling the rest of my body through the hole, I stand up and look around. Twenty kinda, sorta, not-really-see-through me's stare back.

In the shadowy darkness the whole scene is super

disconcerting. I barely swallow the second round of screams that threatens to bubble up.

What I really need is more light.

"You can come through now. It's safe!" I yell. *"I think,"* I add under my breath.

Moments later, Jade, Leroy, and the lantern are at my side.

"Mirrors?" Jade says as she takes in the room's decor. Which is, indeed, composed of nothing but mirrors. We're talking small mirrors. Large mirrors. Round mirrors. Oval mirrors. And even one rectangular monstrosity that's at least as big as an elephant.

"But look, maybe there's more." Leroy gestures almost regretfully toward yet another door.

All is not lost yet!

"Let's see where it goes!" I stick my tongue out at the elephant mirror before sprinting across the room. I ease the door open and reveal . . . the exact same long, boring hallway that we walk down every single day on our way to Room B8.

We're back in the main part of the school.

Leroy exhales in relief.

Jade growls. "I thought for sure we would find *something* useful."

"I did too," I admit. "But why haven't we found this room before? I would have sworn we've gone through every unlocked door in the entire school."

"That's why," Leroy says as the door swings shut behind us. From the mirror room's side, it had looked like any ordinary Ghoul-wood door. But from this side? It's painted *gray*. Which means in the dimly lit hallways of the basement's basement, it blends right in with the stone walls.

As we make our way back upstairs, Jade can't stop grumbling about how anticlimactic everything turned out to be. Neither toys nor mirrors will help us find Josephine's painting. Or a way back home.

But even though I can't argue with her, I can also see a silver lining. Because where there is one secret passageway and one camouflaged door, surely there can be more.

23

Hope Springs Eternal

When I crawl out of bed the next morning, the silver-lining feeling from the night before is still there. In fact, I've got hope pouring out of me in buckets. It's sort of like when you go into a math test armed with your lucky pencil and you just *know* you're going to smash it, even though you didn't study.

Then again, I haven't smashed a math test since the second grade and my "lucky" pencil never seemed all that lucky, so perhaps this isn't the best example. But I feel lucky all the same.

All morning, I keep my eyes peeled for oddly positioned paintings. I don't spot any, but this doesn't diminish my optimism one bit. We still have a slew of hallways we can reexplore, now that we know what we're looking for.

As we sit down for lunch, I study the cafeteria like never before. The mural of nightmares almost touches the ground; could it be concealing another set of stairs? The painting behind Mister Q-tip is too small to be hiding anything bigger than a cat door, but what about the one behind Madam Booth? The frame. . .

That's when I notice it. A glint of tarnished metal peeking out of the tiny pocket inside Madam Booth's skirt. I study the shape, confirming my suspicions.

The metal is from a key.

From *the* key!

Is this the reason I woke up feeling so full of hope? Not because I might find another hidden stairwell, but because I'd soon wind up with a whole new opportunity? Is the gate key's sudden appearance a sign that I should go for it? That the universe *wants* me to turn over a new leaf and become a criminal?

I nudge Jade, who's mood from last night hasn't changed one bit. She's the doom and gloom to my rainbows and deluxe grilled cheese sandwiches. "It's the gate key," I whisper, making sure Leroy—who is knee-deep in an argument with Kevin over what today's lunch smells like, asparagus or cat pee—can't hear. "In Madam Booth's pocket."

Jade's eyes brighten as the meaning of my words slowly penetrate her haze of hopelessness, then they go dull again. "Even if we manage to take it without getting caught, we still don't know where to go. Mister Gruber said it's *a mile* to the nearest thinning, remember? We'll never find it."

Of course I remember, but I'm not letting that stop me. Not this time. Me, seeing the key, today, the same day I wake up feeling so lucky? It's got to be fate. Not that I ever believed in fate before, but I never believed in ghosts before either.

"We will find it, Jade, because we won't stop trying until we do. Think about it. During the day, we can continue our investigation with Leroy, and at night, the two of us can sneak outside and search there. We'll be doubling our chances."

Leroy's heated discussion with Kevin comes to an end (the verdict: lunch smells like fresh asparagus drizzled with a glaze of not-so-fresh cat pee), so I have just enough time to make Jade promise to think about it before Leroy ushers us off to BTBGYCB class. Madam Lecter greets us at the door, the grin on her face massive, even by Madam Lecter standards.

"You're sure in a good mood," Rebecca grumbles. She hates it when other people are happy.

"You're right, I am!" Madam Lecter giggles as she spins and twirls between our desks, her hospital gown flying out behind her like Superman's cape. "My son got engaged last night. Maybe I'll be a grandma soon!"

I'm no good at guessing old people's ages, but Madam Lecter doesn't look like she can be much older than thirty. There isn't a single gray hair, age spot, or saggy wrinkle in sight. Imagining her as a grandma is a weird reminder of how a ghost's appearance never changes. Of how in forty years, Madison will be a puckered, old forty-three-year-old, and I'll still look like a freckly faced kid.

"I'm glad for you, Madam Lecter." Jade's smile looks real, but her voice sounds borderline as sulky as Rebecca's.

Her sulkiness continues when we get to Room B8. Today, Mister Zilla gives us each a deck of cards and tells us to shuffle them, but of course our fingers go straight through the cards. In all the Haunting 101 classes we've had to date, nobody from Table Eight has managed to move an object more than a few millimeters. And one of us (poor Kevin) hasn't moved anything at all.

You'd think Mister Zilla would take our failures as an indication that his style of teaching isn't working, and that maybe he should do something other than scuttle around the room making disapproving comments and exasperated sighs, but he doesn't.

"Ugh, this is pointless!" Jade slams a fist down on the table, but instead of the satisfying *thwack* she was probably hoping for, her hand swooshes straight through the air. Which only makes her madder.

Mister Zilla snakes his way toward us—probably to tell Jade that it is *not* pointless and that she merely needs to "focus more"—but at the last second, he veers off. My guess? Darth Sidious noticed her foul mood and even he got scared.

During free time, Jade harrumphs ten times, sniffles eight times, and kicks the wall five times as she, Leroy, and I explore one of the back stairwells. Honestly, it's almost a relief to join back up with Kevin and Rebecca for dinner, even though the sight of said dinner almost makes me want to kick something myself.

The millisecond Jade's butt meets the chair, she turns to Rebecca and initiates a conversation with her for, what, the first time *ever*?

"Finn and I need your help settling an argument, Rebecca. Though I already know you're going to agree with me and say Finn's a dingbat."

If Rebecca notices the confusion on my face, she shows no hint of it. Always a lover of drama, she agrees at once. In fact, this is the most excited I've seen her since the day I first arrived at Phantom Academy.

"As ghosts, should we be forced to learn reading and writing?"

If Rebecca stopped to think about this question for even a heartbeat, she'd realize that Jade's alleged argument was unequivocal rubbish. Neither Jade nor I have been restrained—*at all*—when it came to expressing our thoughts on the subject. Thoughts that are 100 percent in agreement.

But Rebecca doesn't stop to think. She dives right in with her opinion. "Of course not. When I leave here, I'm planning to read nothing but fashion magazines, and I already know the fashion lingo inside and out."

"What?" Leroy blurts out. "But reading has so many benefits!"

As soon as Leroy hits cruising altitude on his merits-of-reading spiel, Jade whirls around to face me. "I'm in. Let's steal the key." Her fingers tremble slightly as they fiddle with one of the twigs sticking out of her hair. "How about I distract Madam Booth on our way out of the cafeteria, and you nick the key?"

I'm not entirely sure what "nick" means (maybe Leroy has a point about reading, after all), but I can use my context clues as well as the next kid. "How about I do the distracting, and you do the stealing?" I counter back. "I *am* the king of distraction."

Jade bites her lip. "Okay . . . ," she finally agrees.

By the time dinner is over, I've got my diversion all figured out. My inspiration comes from my years of playing soccer, actually. Even though I was never the quickest kid on the team, and even though I was hopelessly outskilled by most first graders, I was an absolute whiz at taking a dive. So why not use that talent now? As we're leaving the dining hall, I'll feign a stumble that will send me soaring right onto the staff table.

Forks will be sent flying. Plates will smash onto the floor. And the small purple Jell-O-like blobs that qualify as tonight's dinner will be sent rolling all over the place—just like the famed meatball sitting on top of spaghetti, all covered with cheese. Considering that Madam Booth is sitting at the far end of the table again tonight, right next to Madam Lecter, the whole thing should be easy-peasy.

It's practically foolproof.

Right?

24
The World Series

When the bell rings to signal the end of dinner, I get up confidently. Instead of beelining it straight into the hallway, I veer off slightly, guiding myself, Jade, and Leroy closer and closer to Madam Booth's corner of the staff table.

For maybe the first time ever, I decide to heed my mom's advice. (Even when everything else about my old life has faded from memory, I'm pretty sure those words—*Think before you act, Finn!*—will remain crystal clear in my head until the day I move on.)

My pace slows as I approach our target, giving my

thinking-before-it-acts brain a chance to catalog the current placement of the forks. The plates. The purple meatball-imitating Jell-O blobs. Instead of throwing myself willy-nilly at the table like I'd normally do, I try to work out the very best launch angle: the one that will lead to maximum impact and give Jade the best shot at carrying out her heist without being spotted.

But the one problem with thinking before you act is that when you give yourself time to think, it gives you time to, well, *think*. And unfortunately, that's exactly what my brain does now. Instead of sticking to launch angles and damage calculations, it starts questioning the whole basis of my plan itself: Do ghosts ever trip?

I mean, we float! We never touch the ground. It's not like our feet can smack into an unseen crack in the sidewalk or get hung up on a stray charging cable or slip on the wet concrete behind the diving board at the YMCA pool.

When I was living among the Living, I didn't need a sidewalk crack to take a nosedive—I often tripped over my own feet—but is this something that *ghosts* do? Since entering the Spirit Realm, have I ever seen a ghost stumble? Have *I* ever stumbled?

Will my ruse be found out immediately?

The staff table is now only four feet away. Jade's eyes

are laser-focused on Madam Booth's pocket, but I'm still paralyzed with questions.

"The World Series game last night was fantastic!"

If I wasn't already frozen in place, Madam Booth's words would have done it. *My dull-as-nails reading and writing teacher likes baseball?* Talk about a curveball!

"There must have been at least a hundred ghosts watching the game from the infield alone, and maybe a thousand more in the outfield. I was right next to the first-base umpire."

As Madam Booth's words sink in, I realize she was AT the game. Not watching it on TV. Not listening to it on the radio. But AT a real, live, actual World Series game.

"There should be another game Friday night, Liv," Madam Booth continues. "That's your night off, isn't it?"

It's not until Madam Lecter nods that I realize *she's* Liv. "I'm planning to check in on my family, same as always, but maybe I'll go to the game afterward. If I feel like it."

The nonchalance of her words hits me like a lava rocket to the chest, and I start seeing red.

Maybe she'll go to a *freaking* World Series game? *If* she feels like it?

Do the teachers somehow not realize how cruel they're being? They go around casually talking about trips home and outings to World Series games when they KNOW the rest of us are trapped inside the school, day after day after day?

The whole system is so colossally unfair, but they don't seem to notice! Or care.

Next to me, Leroy's normally rigid back slumps over till he looks like a palm tree on a super-windy day. No way all this talk about baseball isn't making him think about his brother.

Only Jade seems unaffected as she remains coiled up, ready to jump into action the second my promised diversion materializes. But as the seconds tick by and I do nothing but fume, she eventually relaxes and lets out a huff. "C'mon, guys. Let's go."

The time for my distraction has come . . . and gone. There will be no key stealing tonight. Luckily, the still-slumped-over Leroy is positioned between me and Jade, so at least she can't give me a hard time for my failure. She's forced to keep her annoyance to herself as we trudge out of the cafeteria together. Heads down. Shoulders drooping.

As we randomly take a right turn, Leroy is the first of us to recover. "Should we work on our history homework? It's due tomorrow."

Now Leroy might be the smartest kid I know, but the

fact that there is even the tiniest bit of hope in his voice suggests he hasn't quite figured out me and Jade yet. Of course we don't want to work on homework. We *never* want to work on homework.

"Yeah, that idea gets a giant no," Jade answers for the both of us. "I say we check out the empty wing on the second floor again. I'm sure there's something off about that place."

We float toward the stairwell that will take us to Phantom Academy's weirdly furniture-free rooms. I scrutinize every painting we pass. Same as always.

The Loch Ness Monster pops his head out from under the dark, eerie waters of Loch Ness to blow raspberries at me. A family of mice squeak and chirp as they fly colorful kites in the English countryside. A field of wildflowers makes an entire hallway smell like spring. A grinning bride and groom hold hands in front of a quaint little church.

I drift to a stop in front of the ecstatic couple.

This will be Madam Lecter's son soon—getting married, being happy, having kids. And Madam Lecter will get to know that all these milestones are happening to her family, whereas I'll be kept in the dark about mine. Just like I've been kept in the dark about everything that's happened since the coconut fell.

For instance, did Mom ever get that work promotion she wanted so badly?

No idea.

Did Madison finally get over her fear of butterflies?

No clue.

Did Grandpa ever solve the Rubik's Cube he'd been working on for weeks?

Doubtful, but . . . ?

My hands squeeze into fists as the red-hot lava rockets take aim again. If I could leave the school grounds every once in a while—even if it's only for an hour or so at a time—I *know* I could deal with all the rest. The lectures. The homework. The food. *Being dead.*

In fact, I'm pretty sure I'd come to enjoy it.

But I can't enjoy it now. Not when I'm being caged up like an animal in a zoo.

I make to turn away from the painting—to clear my head before it erupts like Mount Saint Helens—but for some reason, I can't. I lean in closer, suddenly unable to shake the feeling that there is a clue hiding somewhere among the swirls of blue and yellow and pink paint. But what is it?

I don't recognize the church. The newlyweds aren't famous, at least as far as I can tell. And while there is no doubt the groom's baby blue tux is a brave fashion choice, it's not peculiar enough to make my brain tickle. Or to make my I'm-going-to-smash-this-math-test-with-my-lucky-pencil feeling come roaring back.

Perhaps I should strike up a conversation with them?

After making sure Leroy, Jade, and I are alone in the hallway, I smile, I wave, I nod, I tell them congratulations, but the couple is far too busy gazing into each other's eyes to notice I'm there. Their matching lovey-dovey expressions make me want to puke.

"Are you okay, Finn?" Leroy asks.

"Does anything seem strange about this picture?"

Leroy and Jade crowd in next to me.

"Not really," Jade says finally.

I shake my head, but no brilliant thoughts rattle free. "Okay. Let's go, then."

And that's when it hits me like a herd of stampeding elephants; I know what's bugging me about the painting!

Leroy and Jade take off down the hall, but I don't move. I close my eyes and sift through my memories, making sure I'm not way off the mark.

"Ummm, Finn? Are you having a fit or something? Should I get Madam Booth?"

I wave away Jade's questions as my brain finishes puzzling the puzzle pieces together.

It all fits!

"I've got it!" I do a few clumsy pirouettes down the hallway before skipping back. "I know who stole the painting!"

"Wait. What? You do?" Leroy stammers as he looks back at the church and the bride and the groom, trying to find the clue that clued me in.

"I do!"

"It's Mister Zilla, isn't it? Please, please, please say it's Mister Zilla." Jade rubs her hands together like an evil villain.

"I've always thought it would be the headmaster," Leroy says.

"You're both wrong. It was Madam Lecter!"

Jade and Leroy look at me like I've gone and sprouted a pair of fluorescent purple fairy wings. And really, I can't blame them. Up until two minutes ago, I'd have thought it more likely that Bucky the dog stole the painting than Madam Lecter.

"Where's your evidence?" Leroy asks skeptically.

"Madam Lecter said that teachers only get to leave Phantom Academy once a month, right?"

Jade and Leroy nod.

"Then how did she know her son got engaged to be married if her turn to leave school isn't until this Friday?

The timing doesn't fit. She must be leaving Phantom Academy some other way. Some *secret* way."

Leroy's mouth drops open and Jade slaps her forehead. Which—thanks to her ghostly hand and ghostly head—sounds more like a squooshy splat.

"And that's not all. You said Madam Lecter died the day after her only kid was born, right, Jade?"

"Yeah . . ."

"So how come she once complained that she could no longer kiss away his boo-boos or sing him good night? And remember all her funny stories about cleaning up his blowout diapers? I can't believe I didn't notice it before now, but none of that makes any sense. Something is off, way off. I'm just not sure exactly what it is."

Forget about exploring the empty west wing.

Forget about stealing Madam Booth's key.

Forget about our history homework.

It's stakeout time again!

25

Madam Lecter Disappears

Leroy, Jade, and I race back to the dining hall and find that luck is on our side. Madam Lecter is still there, waving goodbye to Madam Booth.

As our BTBGYCB teacher takes off down the hallway, my friends and I go into stealth mode. We hide behind statues, peek around corners, and basically channel our inner mimes as we wordlessly follow in her wake.

Madam Lecter does not make things easy for us, though. Like the cook, she weaves suspiciously through the hallways. Every once in a while, she whirls around suddenly to make sure nobody is behind her. On two occasions she almost spots Leroy, whose stakeout skills are flaming atrocious for someone who reads mystery books all the time.

After what feels like an hour, but is probably only five minutes, Madam Lecter arrives in the basement's basement and walks up to a door. Only it's not just any door.

It's *the* door.

The nearly invisible gray one that leads to the mirror room!

She yanks it open and disappears inside. The door closes silently behind her.

"We *need* to see what's going on in there," Jade whispers.

"Agreed," I respond. Even Leroy nods along.

It takes us a few seconds to locate the gray doorknob in the dim light, but as soon as we do, I ease the door open a few inches. Just far enough for all three of us to peek inside.

Madam Lecter stands in front of the elephant-sized mirror, the same one I stuck my tongue out at yesterday. She tucks a strand of limp hair behind her right ear. She picks at her teeth. She attempts to straighten the creases in her hospital gown, even though it's completely pointless. Same as Jade's wonky glasses, any creases in a ghost's clothing are doomed to remain there forever.

And ever.

And ever.

Apparently satisfied, Madam Lecter squares her shoulders. "Take me to my husband," she tells her reflection, and I almost burst out laughing. Did Madam Lecter notice us following her? Is this her way of messing with us?

If so, well played, Madam Lecter. Well played.

I'm about to step into the room when Jade yanks me back. "Look," she hisses as she tips her head toward the mirror. The surface is now shifting . . . warping . . . distorting . . . until it looks *exactly* like the door to Room B8!

Madam Lecter doesn't hesitate. She walks straight through.

And disappears from view.

Leroy gasps. Jade yelps. I forget how to blink. We all stand there, motionlessly staring at the spot where Madam Lecter had been hovering only moments before.

Finally, I ease into the room and tiptoe over to the mirror, which has gone right back to looking like any other mirror. I tap on the silvery surface with my knuckles. It *feels* like any other mirror too.

"What happened?" Jade asks as she tries, unsuccessfully, to pry the thing off the wall so she can see what's behind it. "How did Madam Lecter walk through this? It's completely solid."

I'm as confused as Jade, but Leroy looks like his brain has switched into overdrive mode. "In our first Haunting 101 class, didn't Mister Zilla say something about how most thinnings of the veil can take you anywhere you want to go?" I nod, not really sure where he is going with this. "Well, what if they also *only appear* when a ghost asks to go somewhere? Maybe they're hidden from view the rest of the time?"

"I don't know about that," Jade says doubtfully. "The doorway to Room B8 always looks funny."

Leroy chews on his lower lip for a moment before responding. "But that thinning only ever goes to one place. I bet that makes a difference."

As his words hit home, excitement rushes into me like I'm a giant helium balloon; I no longer feel like I'm hovering an inch above the ground, but a mile. "So you're saying this mirror is the thinning we've been looking for all along?"

And to think we were standing in this exact same spot only a day ago and had no idea!

"I think so," Leroy says.

"But that means this thing can take us . . . anywhere?"

And I'm hovering right in front of it! All I need to do is say, "Take me home," and in an instant, I'll be with my parents, with Madison, with Scout, my cat.

Jade's body joins mine in the mirrored surface. "We can go home," she says, her voice soft.

"No, no, no, no, no. Wait up, guys." Leroy jumps into action, squeezing himself between us and the mirror. "I want to see my parents and brother too, but we need to be smart here. I don't think we should go off in different directions. We need to stick together."

"Let's rock, paper, scissors for it," Jade suggests. "Winner picks where we go first."

I fist up my right hand, all ready to go (and pick rock, of course—always rock), but Leroy shakes his head. "Weren't either of you listening to Mister Zilla on the first day of class?"

Sure, I listened! To some of it . . .

"He said he'll teach us how to locate the thinnings of the veil right before we graduate. Which probably means that finding them isn't easy. I mean, we'd have never guessed this mirror was a thinning, would we? So if we go through this one right now, we might never be able to find another one. We might be stuck."

And just like that, my helium balloon bursts.

Jade tries to push her way around Leroy. "Then we go

to my house. It's only fair. I've been away from my familia the longest."

But Jade lived in San Jose. I'm from Los Angeles. Without a thinning in the veil to zap us from place to place, it will take forever for me to reach my parents.

Maybe if I'm quick enough and wait for the perfect moment to catch them off guard, I can shove Leroy and Jade out of the way. Then before either of them can stop me, I can say the magic words that will take us to *my* home. Sure, it's a low-down, nasty, devious plan, but what's the alternative? Float four hundred miles? I'd rather eat the cook's food!

Think before you act, Finn.

I try to ignore Mom's mantra, but her words play over and over in my head—*think before you act, think before you act, think before you act*—refusing to let up. I almost stick a finger in each ear, but of course that wouldn't help. The words are *in my head*. Stubbornly refusing to fade away like Dad's shower singing.

I grind my teeth in frustration . . . and then I relent. I will not do that to my friends. Jade and Leroy have been there for me from the very start, supporting me, making me laugh, keeping me from dwelling on everything I've lost. It's only thanks to them that being dead has been tolerable, even fun. And if I'm being completely honest, they're probably the best friends I've ever had.

With all thoughts of backstabbing eradicated from my head, I focus instead on our actual problem: the fact that none of us has a clue how the thinnings work.

What we *really* need is a mentor. A guide. A teacher.

A teacher!

"We can't go to any of our houses," I say, even though the thought kills me. "Not yet. We need to follow Madam Lecter. That way, we can watch how she gets back."

Jade agrees at once, but Leroy's hesitates. His gaze drops to the ground, and I know what he's going to say even before he says it. "I'm not so sure about this anymore, guys. What if Madam Lecter sees us? What if we get in trouble? Maybe we're making a mistake."

But there's no way Leroy's talking me out of this one. "We'll just be walking through a mirror," I reassure him. "And I bet if we read every single rule book that's ever been written in the whole entire history of the world, we'll find there has never, ever been a rule against that."

"Even you have to admit it's the perfect loophole, Leroy," Jade piles on.

I hold my breath as Leroy thinks.

And thinks.

And thinks.

Finally, he looks up. "It's only walking through a mirror." Then he breaks into a huge grin. "Let's go."

Jade fist pumps the air as I thump Leroy on the back, almost as proud of him as I was of Madison when she first learned how to kick a soccer ball.

Our escape plan is back on track.

Neither Jade nor Leroy looks eager to be our group spokesperson, so it's lucky for them that my whole talking-to-the-paintings thing has left me supremely comfortable talking to inanimate objects as though they're alive. I gently move Leroy out of the way and face my reflection.

My kinda, sorta, not-really-see-through body stares back at me. Mom's freckles are sprinkled across my cheeks. Madison's nose is sitting right beneath Dad's hazel eyes. There is even a black Scout hair on my T-shirt, where it will remain for all eternity.

Three words. With three simple words I can see the *real* freckles, the *real* nose, the *real* eyes, the *real* cat.

Jade clears her throat and I quickly shove all thoughts of home out of my head. "Take us to Madam Lecter."

As soon as the words leave my lips, the surface morphs into its soap-bubbly version. I reach back and grab Jade's hand. She grabs Leroy's.

"Don't let go, okay?" I say.

My friends nod. Then we all take a deep breath and step through the bubble, ready to face whatever lies on the other side.

26

The Tunnel

I expect walking through the mirror to be exactly like entering Room B8.

But it's not.

An invisible, clawed hand—or what *feels* like an invisible, clawed hand—grabs ahold of my stomach and pulls,

pulls,

pulls,

me toward... what?

What am I being pulled toward?

Around me are nothing but streaks of white light, flashes of red, and long stretches of nothing but darkness.

The air feels thin and cold as it flies past my face. I squeeze Jade's hand and take strange comfort in Leroy's nearby screams.

Whatever is happening, wherever we're going, I'm glad we're together.

After what feels like a million one-Mississippi's, a circle of light appears ahead. It grows bigger and bigger and bigger as we hurtle toward it. The instant we pass through the ring, a zap shoots through my body—like I've touched a humongous, metal doorknob with a score to settle—and my eyes are assaulted with colors, the like of which I haven't seen in weeks. Rich, dark blues. Vivid reds. All manner of lush greens.

I see tiny houses. Tiny trees. Tiny streetlights.

Jade whoops excitedly, but any impulse I have to revel in our breathtaking bird's-eye view is squashed by the fact that the tiny houses and tiny trees and tiny streetlights are getting bigger. And they're getting bigger fast!

Can a ghost break bones if they slam into the ground hard enough? Based on the newest pitch of Leroy's screams, he's wondering the same thing.

I reluctantly let go of Jade's hand and bring both arms up in front of my face, bracing for impact as the earth barrels closer and closer and closer, until . . .

Oh. Okay. So that wasn't too bad. One second, I'm plummeting through the air at lightning speed; next second, I'm face down in the dirt. If it weren't for the film of mud now coating my tongue, I could almost pretend that I'd been taking a nap in a flower bed.

I roll over, reveling in the fact that nothing hurts. I must have slammed into the ground *hard* for my body to have actually made contact before returning to its normal inch-above-the-ground position, and yet I never felt a thing.

A laugh bubbles up from my stomach. We've made it! We've found a way out of the school!

But the laugh quickly dies as I crawl to my feet and realize Jade and Leroy are not crawling to their feet next to me. I spin in a circle.

Where are they?

Fear closes in on me as I whirl around and around and around. Each circle confirms the same truth: I'm completely and categorically alone.

"Leroy? Jade?" Panic makes my voice wobble worse than the bobblehead doll on the dashboard of Grandpa's car.

Where could they be? When I let go of Jade's hand, did I zoom off in one direction while she and Leroy zoomed off in another?

A sound comes from somewhere to my right, and my

head whips to the side. My ears tell me someone is spewing their guts out in the bushes, by my eyes tell me nobody is there.

Not a person. Not an animal. *Nothing*.

If I were still alive, I'd die of fright right here. Right now.

I don't know where I am. I don't know what happened to my friends. I don't know how to get back to where I came from.

My head is spinning with worst-case scenarios when *bam*! Something smacks into me, and we both topple to the ground. Except the "something" is actually "nothing."

There. Is. Nothing. There!

And yet I can feel it on top of me. And it's *laughing*.

"Wow, you scare easy, Finn," the Nothing says.

"Jade?"

"Yes, of course it's me. We go nearly invisible in the Land of the Living, remember?"

No. I *hadn't* remembered. Obviously.

Slowly my body relaxes, and my brain starts working. "So that means the puking person is—"

"Yup, it was me," comes Leroy's disembodied voice. "Sorry about that."

My eyes slowly adjust to being in the Land of the Living, just like they do every time I enter Room B8, and Jade and Leroy come into sharper focus. Leroy stands to my left, clutching his stomach. Jade is running full steam toward a huge oak tree. I gasp as she disappears ... and pops out the other side a nanosecond later.

"This is a-m-a-z-i-n-g!" she yells as she turns around and traverses the tree again, this time in slow motion.

My face cracks into the biggest smile I've smiled in weeks. In no time, all three of us are running around like farts in a mitten as we whiz through trees. Moonwalk through cars. Somersault through fences.

"What do you think will happen if I run through that moth?" Jade asks.

Without waiting for an answer, she takes off. I watch, mesmerized, as her nearly-see-through body collides with the insect and *goes straight through*. The moth's wings stop flapping and it drops one foot, two feet, three feet. It's about to hit the grass when its wings finally move again, and off it shoots toward the nearest lamppost.

I let out a cheer. Mister Moth will not be entering the Spirit Realm tonight!

"Hey, guys?" Leroy says, interrupting my happy dance. "Where do you think we are?"

I rotate slowly, really taking in our surroundings for

the first time. We're in a quiet neighborhood filled with small, brightly colored houses, majestic oak trees, and white picket fences.

"I have no idea, but please tell me one of you remembers where we landed. I was too excited to pay attention," Jade says nervously.

"I was too busy vomiting," Leroy admits.

"And I was too busy freaking out." I force myself to concentrate, to remember, to ignore the newest wave of terror threatening to take over.

Dirt! Even now, I can still feel the gritty grains on my tongue. I look around again, this time with purpose. "There." I point to a large flower garden in front of a yellow Victorian. "I think I plopped down there."

Leroy nods slowly. "Okay. That sounds about right. I was probably puking in those bushes."

I float toward the yellow house. This must be where Madam Lecter's husband lives. This must be where my teacher spends every single night—when she isn't in the mood to attend World Series games, that is.

"Let's take a peek inside," Jade suggests.

We drift over to a tall, skinny window that looks into a cozy living room. There isn't a person or ghost or animal in sight.

"This is boring," I say. "Let's go in."

Ignoring Leroy as he panics over privacy and trespassing—"What if we get arrested?"—I step closer to the yellow siding.

Then I take one more step, and I'm on the other side.

27

Talking to Mailboxes

I'm immediately drawn to the side table next to the couch. It's covered with photographs.

There's a youngish Madam Lecter with her arm around the waist of a man with kind eyes and a warm smile.

There is Madam Lecter in a wedding gown, looking like the happiest woman alive as she says "I do" to the kind-eyed man.

There is a slightly older Madam Lecter in a hospital gown. Pale and exhausted, she gazes adoringly at the tiny baby sleeping in her arms.

And then Madam Lecter disappears from the photos.

The man and the baby grow older and older and older, but it's always only the two of them. At the beach. At the zoo. At the boy's graduation.

The pictures pierce my heart.

"Let's check out the rest of the house," Jade whispers, and I happily turn my back on the table of sadness.

We walk down a short hallway, past a bathroom, past a dining room. We slow as we approach the kitchen, which smells *amazing*. Like my dad's slow cooker beef stew.

Eventually, a man comes into view. He's standing at a counter, peeling carrots. When he turns his head slightly, I recognize him as the man from the photos.

Only now his hair is grayer. And there's a lot less of it.

"I told them Lake Tahoe could be chilly in October, but they insist on having the wedding there anyway," the man says to someone I can't yet see.

Jade places a finger against her lips, and we tiptoe forward. Based on what we learned in BTBGYCB class, Madam Lecter's husband shouldn't be able to see us. He also shouldn't be able to hear us, so long as we don't go banging pots and pans together or screaming our heads off. Which of course we won't do.

Because we've got brains and everything.

Not even a second after that thought crosses my mind, Leroy goes and SCREAMS!

And honestly, I almost scream too.

Because the person Madam Lecter's husband is talking to? It's Madam Lecter herself!

Not only that, but Madam Lecter has done whatever Mister Zilla does to make himself visible in Room B8. Mister Lecter can actually *see* his dead wife's kinda, sorta, not-really-see-through body!

Warty warthogs, our BTBGYCB teacher is majorly breaking the rules of ghosthood. The rules *she* taught us.

Thanks to Leroy's scream, two heads swing in our direction. Mister Lecter squints at an area of the room about two feet to the left of where we're standing, but Madam Lecter's gaze fixes on us immediately. Her eyes widen with shock. Then narrow with anger.

"C'mon," I hiss at Jade and Leroy, and we take off. Not bothering with hallways, we tear straight through the walls, the doors, the furniture, a fish tank filled with five colorful fish and one not-so-colorful snail.

We need to get back to Phantom Academy—quick—before Madam Lecter catches us. She might be the nicest teacher in the whole entire school, but it's not like we caught her eating with her mouth open or forgetting to wash her hands after going to the bathroom. We caught her doing something majorly illegal. Something that—if we tell anyone—might lead to her being forced to move on.

How far will Madam Lecter go to ensure we don't tell?

Will she lock us in a dungeon? Superglue our mouths shut? Feed us a constant supply of übersticky caramels? Or will she pull a Sir Arthur and do whatever Sir Arthur George Cunningham III did to silence his sister?

Leroy, Jade, and I race straight for the flower garden and skid to a stop. Looking around.

There is no mirror here. No door. No shimmery, soap-bubble-like surface.

It's exactly as Leroy had predicted. The way back is precisely as clear as our kitchen window that time Madison painted all over it with peanut butter.

"What do we do?" Jade asks.

"I don't know!" Leroy's arms start flailing like he's imitating Rex from *Toy Story*.

I take a few deep breaths. *Think*, Finn, *think*!

I can only come up with one idea. I look at the dirt by my feet. "Take us to Phantom Academy."

A mouse scurries between a daisy and a pansy, but nothing else happens. The ground doesn't shift or warp or change.

"Take us back to Phantom Academy," I tell the closest tree.

The dark brown bark remains as solid as ever.

Around me, Jade and Leroy start doing the same. Before long, we've asked every plant, shrub, and mailbox within twenty feet of where we landed to magic us back home, but Nothing Is Happening.

"Wait, what's that sound?" Jade asks.

I wave goodbye to the fire hydrant that I was trying to have a conversation with and listen. Someone is crying. Someone inside Madam Lecter's house.

We float back to the front window and peak inside. Our BTBGYCB teacher's arms are wrapped around her husband. Her kinda, sorta, not-really-see-through forearms sink several inches into his back. Tears stream down the man's face. The sobbing sound comes from Madam Lecter.

Leroy, Jade, and I turn away. I don't know what's going on in there, but it doesn't feel right to watch.

Dejected, we withdraw from the house to discuss our next steps. Leroy argues that we should hide under the neighbor's orange pickup truck and watch what Madam Lecter does when she comes out, but this seems way too risky to me. What if she walks in the other direction and we can't see where she stops? Or what if we can't hear the words she uses? We could wind up stranded in the Land of the Living forever.

Leroy seems ready to take this risk . . . until I remind him that he hasn't learned how to pick up a book yet.

Finally, we agree. Our best bet is to wait for Madam Lecter to finish whatever she's doing, come outside, and deliver her sentence. Will it be the übersticky caramels . . . or something worse?

We trudge over to the flower garden and flop down amid the blooms. The smell of dirt and flowers and someone grilling hot dogs up the street envelops me. If I close my eyes, ignore Leroy's nervous fidgeting, and make my brain go fuzzy, I can almost hear my dad calling me inside for dinner. Hear my mom's awful classical music waft out from an open window. Hear Madison's ecstatic squeals as she rides her tricycle up and down the sidewalk.

And suddenly, I'm struck with the most spectacular thought. If Madam Lecter can show herself to her husband—and presumably to her son, too, being that she'd ran her fingers through his hair and kissed his boo-boos and changed his diapers, events that now make a whole lot more sense—then I can do the same. And based on what Madam Lecter told us on the first day of BTBGYCB class, and what I just witnessed inside her kitchen, if we make ourselves visible to the Living, they'll be able to hear us too.

A new plan for my ghost life begins solidifying in my mind. One where I'm not *watching* my family, but I'm actually a part of it again. Where we can hold actual conversations and play actual games. Where I can give Madison piggyback rides. Eat ice cream with Grandpa. Hug Mom. And scarf down a few dozen of Dad's chocolate chip cookies without worrying that Madison will get blamed for their disappearance.

For this plan to become reality, though, first I need to return to Phantom Academy and learn *how* to turn myself visible. And this will only happen if my BTBGYCB teacher lets me and Leroy and Jade go back to school in the first place, instead of shipping us off to live with Santa and his elves in the North Pole.

Even though I'm still lost in daydream land, I can sense when Leroy's fidgeting morphs into full-on squirming. I open my eyes and quickly discover what has him so nervous: We're moments away from ascertaining our fate.

Madam Lecter is heading our way.

28
It All Comes Out

I'm not sure what I'm expecting, but it isn't for Madam Lecter to sit in the flower garden right next to us, her body back to being as near-invisible as ours. The crack in her voice as she says "Hello" is the only indication that moments ago she'd been wailing into her husband's arms.

"You kids gave me quite a shock, showing up in my kitchen like that. I thought preventing you, Finn, from talking to Josephine's painting would be the end of it, and yet here you all are. Care to tell me how you figured things out?"

From the expressions on Jade's and Leroy's faces, they're

every bit as confused as I am. We'd been expecting Madam Lecter to come outside and do something awful to us, but instead she's acting like her normal, nice self.

Is it an act?

Can we trust her?

After thinking for a minute, I can't see a reason to hold back. No matter what we say, she'll do what she wants to do. We're at her mercy.

So I start talking, with Jade and Leroy jumping in from time to time with their own versions of events.

"Wow, I'm impressed," Madam Lecter says when we're done. "After you graduate, you three should consider a job in the crime-solving branch of the GGA."

Jade and I share a look. "The GGA?" I finally ask.

"The Ghostly Governmental Agency," Leroy answers, rolling his eyes. "It formed after the third ghost war. Don't you remember? Mister Gruber lectured about it for almost an entire class."

Jade and I share another look. Maybe I pay less attention in class than I thought...

But regardless, Madam Lecter's suggestion does have some merit. If I ever get bored living with my parents and watching movies and going on the Rise of the Resistance ride at Disneyland over and over again, crime solving with the GGA might be a nice way to pass a few hours.

That's when it hits me. Madam Lecter implied we'd *have* a life (A death? An existence?) after school. Does that mean she's not about to maroon us on a desert island in the middle of the North Pacific?

"What's going to happen to me and Leroy and Jade now?" I ask, crossing my fingers.

Madam Lecter seems puzzled by the question. "What will happen to you? I take you back to school."

Jade frowns dubiously, but it's Leroy who speaks next. "Why are you breaking the rules, Madam Lecter?"

Leave it to Leroy to ask about rules.

Madam Lecter sighs, and then it's her turn to tell a story.

"I'm not really sure where to begin, so I guess I'll start with my death. When I died just twenty-four hours after my son was born, I was filled with rage. My husband and I hadn't even settled on a name for him yet, and already he'd been stolen from me. That's why I chose the dark, dreary path through the woods instead of the one that cut through the field of flowers; it matched my mood.

"The moment I became a ghost, I was taken to the Spirit Institute—one of the schools meant for adults. While there, my anger and grief only intensified. The four months I was trapped inside the institute felt like an eternity; all I wanted was to see my child again."

My jaw tightens slightly. Of course I feel bad for Madam Lecter, but still! She's complaining about four months. Try five *years*!

"Finally, I graduated. Ignoring the multitudes of warnings given by my school that we should wait a while before returning home, I raced straight back to my family. But my long-anticipated homecoming did not go as I'd expected. Night after night, I watched my husband struggle to care for an infant, all while simultaneously mourning my death. This man I loved more than anyone on the planet—besides my son, whom he named Bradly, after my dad—wasn't sleeping. He wasn't eating. He was about to get fired from his job. He was losing his will to live."

Madam Lecter closes her eyes and takes several deep breaths. With her pale skin and hospital gown, I'd often thought of Madam Lecter as weak. But for her to stay by her husband, watching as he was eaten away by grief when she could easily have run away to a beach or mountain or World Series game? She must be tougher than Kevlar!

"Like you, Leroy, I've always been a rule follower. So I followed the rules of ghosthood to a T, even though it was torture. But then one night, when Bradly was being especially colicky as he kicked and screamed in my husband's arms, Jim looked straight into the corner of the room where I was floating. I'll never, ever forget the hopelessness I saw in his eyes. And you know what he said?"

"What?" Jade asks breathlessly. "What did he say?"

"He said, 'I need you, Liv. Please come back.'"

Jade clutches at her chest like it's just been ripped in two. "What did you do?"

"I forgot about the rules, about the consequences of breaking them, about all of it. Jim, my husband, was the only thing that mattered. I showed myself."

Then Madam Lecter does the very last thing I'd ever expect her to do: She laughs. A full-on, side-splitting, would-probably-bring-tears-to-her-eyes-if-ghosts-could-cry laugh.

"Jim screamed so loud, I'm pretty sure the astronauts on the space station heard him. He screamed so loud, Bradly *stopped* screaming, probably out of pure shock. But once he calmed down, and I explained the situation, we started a new life together. It was nothing like what we'd expected our lives to be like when we got married, but it worked for us. For a while."

Madam Lecter tells us how she was unusually lucky, and no other ghosts lived inside her house. This meant that as long as she stayed within the four yellow walls, she could show herself 100 percent of the time. She could go about her death acting, as much as possible, as though she were still alive.

She rocked Bradly to sleep at night.

She changed his diapers.

She kissed his boo-boos.

She vacuumed and dusted and spent countless hours vegging in front of the television.

Everything was wonderful . . . at first. But slowly, the guilt crept in. Growing and growing until it consumed her.

"But why did you feel guilty, Madam Lecter?" I ask. She was basically living my dream, apart from the vacuuming and dusting and changing diapers bit. "You were with your family. Wasn't everybody happy?"

"Well, yes and no. We *were* happy, but I could also see the toll my presence was taking on Jim and Bradly. By being there, I kept them from moving on. From living their full lives. The lives they deserved."

This made zero sense to me. How could Madam Lecter sitting on the couch watching TV possibly keep her family from living?

Madam Lecter must see the bewilderment on my face,

because she answers my question without me saying a word.

"They were stuck, you see? My husband hardly ever left the house, apart from going to work. Bradly could never invite friends over because I might accidentally pop through a wall and scare them to death. They had to keep my entire existence a secret from everyone, including my heartbroken parents. They had to watch every word they ever spoke."

Madam Lecter swallows hard, her voice now nothing but a whisper. "And my husband could never date, never get remarried, never have another child. I'd sentenced him to a life among the dead."

"Whoa," Jade breathes. "That really sucks."

Madam Lecter nods, but I'm still not sure. If I suddenly returned home to my family and showed myself, they'd be nothing but happy. My parents, my sister, my grandparents, they love me. I'm sure they'd want me around.

"Eventually, I couldn't stand it anymore," Madam Lecter says, bringing me back to her story. "Even though it was agonizing, I said goodbye to my family and took a teaching post at Phantom Academy. I knew the job only allowed teachers to enter the Land of the Living once a month. I'd be forced to let my family go."

Or so she thought.

"How did you figure out about the secret exit?" Leroy asks, his eyes as round and glittery as the streetlight that just popped on behind him. "Can you talk to the paintings like Finn?"

"I wish," she says, flashing me a quick smile, "but no. I don't have that skill. Rather, when I arrived at the school, I was given Josephine Cunningham's old office. One day, as I was digging through some old books and papers, I found her journal. It told all about the secret exit. I took this as a sign that I was *meant* to go back to my family, though deep down I knew I was simply looking for any excuse to go back. I missed them so much."

Mustache Lady had a journal? I'd play charades with Mister Zilla every night for a month if it meant I could read through it just once.

"Does the journal say what happened to Josephine?" I ask eagerly. "Where she went?"

Madam Lecter shakes her head sadly. "It does not. The last entry mentioned that her brother had discovered the truth of her deception, and he'd flown into a rage. Josephine was clearly petrified. She wrote nothing after that."

I shiver at the thought of Mustache Lady facing off

against an angry Sir Arthur George Cunningham III. Even when trapped inside a painting, the man is terrifying.

Next to me, Leroy starts getting antsy again, probably because the sky is darkening fast. It must be getting close to lights-out time back at school.

Madam Lecter climbs to her feet and gives us a quick lesson on how to locate the thin spots in the veil. It's no wonder we never found one ourselves. Instead of *seeing* the thinnings, you *feel* them; the air gets lighter and colder the closer you get.

"I know it's hard to detect them now," Madam Lecter says, "but trust me. With a little practice, you'll be able to feel any natural thinning of the veil from blocks away. The ghost-made ones—like the mirror at school—are different, of course. Those you can only find if you know where they are."

Madam Lecter stands in the spot where she *claims* the feelings of coldness and lightness are the strongest—but which feels exactly like every other spot to me—and asks to be transported to the mirror room in Phantom Academy. Almost at once, a soap-bubble surface appears in the middle of the street.

Leroy's face turns a shade greener as he moves toward the portal, like the mere thought of traveling back through the veil is making him sick. Before any of us can step through, though, our BTBGYCB teacher holds out an arm. Stopping us.

"As you may have overheard, before I left my house, I told my husband goodbye for good. I asked him to tell Bradly that I love him, and I urged them both to move on with their lives. It will be difficult, very difficult, but this time I'm staying away for good. When we get back to school, I'm hoping the three of you will keep my actions here a secret. But ultimately, that's up to you."

Finished speaking, Madam Lecter drifts forward and whooshes out of sight. Leroy, Jade, and I once again hold hands.

And we jump in after her.

By the time the mirror spits us into the basement's basement, Leroy has two hands clamped over his mouth. "We'd better hurry," he says through clenched teeth, his face even greener than before. "I bet we only have ten minutes until lights out."

"You two go on ahead. I'll be right behind you," I tell my friends.

Jade hesitates, but I motion for her to leave. I have one more thing I need to ask Madam Lecter.

As soon as we're alone, I turn to my teacher. "Did

Josephine's journal say anything about her ability to talk to the paintings? About her seeing them move?" For some reason, I hold my breath as I wait for the answer.

"She wrote about that a lot."

Relief floods my body. The rumors were true. I'm not the only one. I'm not sure why, but I find that comforting.

"Did she say *how* she could talk to the paintings, when nobody else could?"

Madam Lecter shakes her head. "She never figured it out, but she did have a couple of guesses. One guess was that she was hallucinating the whole thing."

I gasp, and Madam Lecter chuckles. "I think we can rule out hallucinations now, considering you have the same gift. Her second guess was that the paintings in the Spirit Realm move and talk all the time, but only the very rare person has the ability to see it. Like how some people can do outrageously complex math problems in their heads."

A rare ability? Now *that* I can handle.

"If I had to guess, there are a lot of other ghosts like you. Some probably even attended Phantom Academy; they were just a little less loose-lipped about their abilities than you've been. If you want, I can put feelers out to some teachers I know at other schools."

My Cheshire-cat grin is all the answer Madam Lecter needs. "Who knows," she says with a wink. "Maybe there is a secret society out there, just for people like you."

As I start daydreaming about joining some covert club, Madam Lecter makes for the door. "Why don't you go on to bed now, Finn. I have a painting to return."

29
Reality SUCKS

Twenty minutes after lights out, there's a knock on Leroy's and my door.

"It's me," Jade whispers from the other side. "Let me in."

Leroy bolts upright. "I'm not sure we're allowed—" he starts, but he doesn't bother finishing his sentence. Probably because I've already opened the door.

And Jade's already halfway to planting herself on my bed.

"We're keeping Madam Lecter's secret a secret, right?" Jade doesn't even bother to look at me; her eyes focus only on Leroy. "She might have broken a major rule, but

I don't think she deserves to be moved on for it."

Leroy picks at his fingernails as he considers his answer. Finally, he gives his never-going-away hangnails a break. "I agree. I think she's learned her lesson."

"I agree too," I add, just in case there is any doubt. "Especially since I'm going to break the exact same rule as soon as I can. The minute we're taught how, I'm showing myself to my family."

Leroy's the one I expect to jump down my throat, but it's Jade who cries out first. "Really? Are you serious? I don't think I could do that to my familia."

"What do you mean you couldn't do that to them? Don't you think they'd want to see you? Wouldn't it make them happy?" I always thought Jade got along super well with her family—excluding her sister María, of course.

"Sure they'd be happy, at first, but weren't you listening to Madam Lecter? Eventually, it would royally mess up their lives."

Jade sounds so sure of herself, but she's talking nonsense. Doesn't she realize that our situation is nothing like Madam Lecter's? We don't have kids or husbands. It's not like our appearance would suddenly make someone never get married or never have more children or anything.

Leroy must sense my misgivings, because he quickly

springs to Jade's aid. "Can't you see how hard it would be for them to keep us a secret, Finn?"

"Not really," I admit. I'm good at keeping secrets. Like the fact that I know where Mom's hidden candy stash is. Or the D- I once got on a geography pop quiz.

"I think it would be awful," Leroy says. "Once my parents planned a surprise party for my nana, and I was so afraid I'd blow the whole thing that I started getting stomachaches. If I had to keep it a secret that I had *a ghost living in my house*? I think I'd have died."

"And my abuela has a bad heart," Jade piles on. "I bet she'd have a heart attack if I suddenly showed up at home."

Leroy starts talking again, but his words can't get past my hands, which are now pressed tight against my ears. I don't want to hear any of this.

The moment I learn how to make myself visible, I'm doing it. 100 percent.

I don't want to *watch* my dad make his amazing homemade pizzas; I want to make the pizzas with him.

I don't want to *watch* Madison play Barbies. For some strange, inexplicable reason, I want to be the one in charge of pushing the hot pink convertible around the living room.

And I can already see the smile that will spread across Mom's face when she sees me for the first time. Once she gets over her shock and stops screaming her guts out, that is.

But even as my hands keep out any new words, the ones Jade and Leroy have already said are still there. Creeping around inside my skull. Slithering in and out of my brain.

Jade and Leroy might think their appearance would mess up their family's lives, but that wouldn't happen to mine. My family can handle it.

I mean, sure, it might be a little hard at first because of Madison. She says anything and everything that pops into her head, so zero chance she's keeping quiet about her big brother the ghost. Either Mom or Dad will probably need to quit their job and stay home with her, rather than risk daycare.

And I suppose Mom will never want to go out for dinner or go on vacations or go to the movies anymore, because she won't want to leave me home alone. I'll offer to tag along and stay quiet and invisible the entire time, but knowing her, she'll hate that too.

And gosh. If Jade's grandma would have a heart attack at the sight of Jade, might Grandma Winters have another stroke when she sees me?

Could I KILL my grandma?

My hands fall to my sides, and Jade's voice immediately

pierces the silence. ". . . and my house is about a million years old. I bet at least a dozen ghosts already call the place home. So even if I *wanted* to pull a Lecter, there's no way I wouldn't get caught."

"I live in an old house too," I admit. "Maybe my plan won't work, after all."

Jade puts a squishy ghost arm around my shoulder. "I'm disappointed too, Finn."

"We all are," Leroy admits. "But don't forget that a few hours ago, all we wanted was to find a way out of here so we could *see* our families. And we've found that way out. We've gotten our wish."

Leroy makes a great point, but the victory feels hollow, now that I know there was an alternative.

"Except after hearing what Madam Lecter went through when she first went home," Leroy continues, "I'm no longer sure I'm ready to see my parents quite yet."

"Me neither," Jade says. "This morning I'd have given anything to go home, but now I'm not sure that's what I want. Even though it's been months, I bet my family is still really sad."

Leroy picks at an invisible speck on his pants. "Yeah, I don't think I can bear to see my mom and dad crying because of me."

That's when I realize that in most of my daydreams of going home, I've imagined my family like they were before my death. Dad cooking. Madison playing. Mom rooting for me from the sidelines of a soccer game.

In reality? They're probably still a total mess. Can I really watch them weep over my death, knowing I can't do anything to cheer them up?

A silence deeper than Crater Lake falls upon the room. It stretches on for minutes, if not hours, before Leroy finally shatters it. "We still have each other."

Jade—who's been lying face down on my bed—flips around. "You're right, Leroy. And maybe if we stop spending so much time dreaming about our old lives, we'll be more alive here. Like, I'd really love to explore the garden again. And study those spiders we found yesterday in that hidden stairwell. And maybe even spend some time in the library?"

I gasp in mock horror at the thought of Jade *wanting* to go to a place full of books, while Leroy puffs out his chest. "If you don't watch out, soon you'll be wishing *you'd* died while wearing a READ MORE BOOKS! T-shirt. If I'm remembering correctly, it also came in pink, blue, red, yellow, gray, and black."

"It came in all those colors, and you picked *maroon?*" Jade laughs.

"Hey, wait a minute, you two." I interrupt their conversation before it can escalate into a full-blown battle of the colors. "I just thought of something. Maybe we aren't ready to go to our houses quite yet, but that doesn't mean we can't use Josephine's secret exit to go other places."

Jade's feet begin thumping excitedly against my mattress. "You're right! Except I don't think I could feel a thinning of the veil if one materialized right in front of me. I had no clue what Madam Lecter was talking about when she was showing us how to find them."

"I didn't get it either," I admit, "but I bet she'd give us another lesson if we ask. She doesn't want us to become stranded in the Land of the Living; that could lead to some major awkwardness."

Jade's eyes are every bit as glittery as the disco balls hanging from the ceiling three floors below us. "And once she's done teaching us, we'll be able to go anywhere we want. Like Maui!"

"Or the Great Wall of China," Leroy suggests.

"We can ride on every single roller coaster in the world."

"And visit the Insectropolis in New Jersey."

"And explore the aqueducts in Rome!"

"And we can watch a real live European soccer—I mean football—game in Wembley Stadium!"

In other words, all of the Land of the Living will be ours to explore.

30

Mustache Lady Returns

The next morning, I crawl out of bed extra early. Leroy does too, but our reasons are very different. Leroy wants to finish the history assignment he never got to last night because we were too busy talking to mailboxes and solving mysteries.

And me? I have a painting to talk to.

When I step into the hallway, it's immediately obvious that Mustache Lady is back. Not only does the air no longer smell like pipe smoke, but it echoes with Josephine's all-too-familiar snores.

It takes three ahems, two coughs, and four claps before her eyes flutter open.

"Hello, Miss Josephine. My name is Finn."

Mustache Lady's mustache curves up in a smile, but she just sits there—looking and listening—for what feels like ages before she says anything back. "Good morning, Master Finn. How wonderful to finally meet you."

"My friends and I found your exit last night."

The corner of her eyes crinkle. "You did? How very clever of you. I presume you know to keep silent about the mirror, at least for now?"

"We won't say a word," I promise.

Even as Mustache Lady nods in approval, her face becomes serious. "I let my excitement get the better of me when you first arrived, Master Finn, when I kept recklessly trying to speak with you. I apologize for that. Moving forward, I will be more careful, and I counsel you to do the same. You should endeavor, always, to keep your ability to communicate with the Spirit Realm paintings a secret."

"But why?"

"Because people fear anything that's different or unknown, and fear, unfortunately, can make people do awful things. I do not want you getting hurt."

Whoa, so Josephine thinks it might be *dangerous* for

people to know what I can do? Could this be why Unicycle Man always seemed so reluctant to speak to me? Was he trying to protect me?

Even though I find it borderline ridiculous that anyone could feel threatened by a kid who talks to pictures, I suppose fear doesn't always make sense. After all, my sister is afraid of *butterflies*.

"I've already let it slip what I can do," I tell Mustache Lady at last, "but I'll be more careful from now on."

"That's all I can ask. The wake-up bell will ring soon, but I am so pleased to have made your acquaintance. It has been over a decade since I've been able to converse with anyone. It gets lonely."

A *decade*? But didn't Josephine disappear in the 1700s? The math doesn't add up. Unless . . .

"Have you met others like us?" Was Madam Lecter right?

"Only a handful, but I fancy the number would have been much higher had my good-for-nothing brother not stuck my portrait in a spot where hardly a sole ever crosses my path."

I open my mouth, but Josephine shushes me. A few seconds later, two boys float down the main hallway, joking about what they'd just left in the toilet.

"It was so green and gloppy!"

"I know! My poops were like little green golf balls."

Neither of them notices me, but Josephine remains on high alert until they're completely out of sight.

At which point the bell rings and more doors open.

I have a ton more questions I want to ask her—like what her brother did to her and if she knows where the real Josephine is right now—but those questions will have to wait.

"You ready?" Leroy asks. At some point he must have left our bedroom, and I didn't even notice.

"Yeah, let's go."

Given the events of the previous few days—all the highs, the lows, the rock bottoms—I'm not quite sure how the day will go. But I try to do exactly what Jade said last night. Instead of obsessing over thoughts of home, I focus on what's right in front of me.

I take a teeny-tiny bite of the shiny, mustard-yellow, sausage-shaped thing that the cook deposits on my plate at breakfast, then joke with Kevin about the taste.

I air-skip all the way to Room 11, earning myself a huge grin from Pink Dress Girl.

I hold open the classroom door for Rebecca and laugh as she gives me some majorly serious side-eye.

The Spirit Realm colors might be as muted as ever, but today everything looks just a little bit brighter.

It actually reminds me a lot of when I went to a sleep-away camp last summer. I was so homesick the first night that I called home, begging my parents to come get me. Mom said I had to stick it out for one more day, and if I was still miserable, she'd pick me up. Her caveat: I had to at least *try* to have fun.

Well, the next morning I made a new friend. Then I learned how to canoe. Then I got a bull's-eye in archery. Then I made a second friend. And by dinner, I was having an amazing time. It wasn't that I suddenly stopped missing home, but I did stop thinking about it all the time.

At the end of the week, I thought Mom might be a little sad, or hurt, that I'd decided not to leave camp early. But she hadn't been sad at all. In fact, she'd been *proud* of me.

Would she be proud of me now, too, if she knew I was choosing NOT to visit home?

I can't help but smile as I realize that even without my lucky pencil, I've never been more certain of an answer in my entire life—or afterlife.

31

Jade Swallows a Jackrabbit

"Pull out your free-writing journals," Madam Booth instructs as we near the end of writing class. Upon hearing these words, Rebecca finally stops giving me the side-eye—Was it *that* odd that I held the door open for her?—so she can roll her eyes at Madam Booth instead. "You have ten minutes. Make the most of it."

For the first time ever, I don't groan my usual groan at the mention of free writing. Instead, I flip through my notebook, passing nothing but doodles.

There are doodles of soccer balls, which basically look like circles filled with giant polka dots.

There are doodles of chocolate chip cookies. Which, come to think of it, are pretty indistinguishable from the soccer balls.

There are doodles of Mister Zilla in a Darth Sidious cloak, wielding a lightsaber. Doodles of cats. Doodles intended to look like portals to the Land of the Living. Even a couple of doodles of Bucky the dog.

The one thing missing from my journal?
Words.
But today that changes.

Things I Never Want to Forget About My Mom

- Her hair smells like oranges.
- She snorts when she laughs.
- She's a TERRIBLE cook.
- She gives the best hugs.
- Her farts could KILL A RHINO!
- She was always there for me, no matter what.

I scribble furiously for the entire ten minutes, making lists for Mom and Dad and Madison. Even though I've decided I'm done spending all my time looking backward, I don't want to forget. Not ever.

"Madam Booth?" Jade says when the bell rings,

marking the end of class. "Can I start going outside during free time?"

On the far side of the room, Kevin perks up as Madam Booth considers Jade's question. "There's always been an unspoken rule that students cannot leave the school, but I'm not entirely sure why this is. I will discuss the topic with Headmaster Cunningham at lunch and pass along your request."

"I want to go outside also," Kevin says. "Can you pass on my request too?"

Madam Booth chuckles, probably for the first time in her death. "I will. I think it would be nice to see the school grounds full of children."

As we head to the cafeteria after history class, Jade sidles up to Kevin. "I didn't know you liked the outdoors."

"Like the outdoors? I *love* the outdoors!"

"Really? Then why haven't you said anything before? I talk about going outside all the time."

Kevin shakes his head. "No, you don't. You talk about *bugs* all the time."

Jade looks like she's about to argue, but my laughter cuts her off. "He's totally right, Jade. You basically never talk about going outside unless you're also talking about beetles or spiders or some other creepy-crawly thing."

"And I don't really like bugs," Kevin admits. "I'm more of a plant person."

"I'm not entirely sure what to make of people who don't like bugs, but still. If we get permission to go outside, you should totally explore the garden with us." Jade motions for Kevin to take the seat next to her at Table Eight, and before long, they're engrossed in conversation about hiking and camping and geocaching. By the end of lunch, even Kevin's plate still sits untouched.

Kevin joins us for the trek to BTBGYCB class, but when we arrive, he sneaks off to his usual desk. We invite him to move closer, but he shakes his head. "That was fun, and I definitely want to go to the garden with you, but I need to be alone for a bit."

"Where's Madam Lecter?" Leroy wonders aloud as the bell rings and the front of the room stays empty. One minute passes.

Two minutes.

Three minutes.

When Madam Lecter finally drifts through the door ten minutes into the period, she looks equal parts lost and miserable. Not only are her eyes dull, but her hallmark smile is missing.

"Are you okay, Madam Lecter?" Kevin asks.

"I will be." Madam Lecter sighs. "I had a rough night, is all."

Instead of teaching something new, she gives us a handout and tells us to work on it for the remainder of the hour.

As soon as Rebecca and Kevin become absorbed in the assignment, Jade, Leroy, and I cautiously approach Madam Lecter's desk. We find her gazing wistfully at a photograph of her husband and son.

"I'm sorry we caused you to lose all that." I motion toward the picture. It's been hard enough having my family snatched away once; I can't imagine going through it again.

"It wasn't your fault. If anything, I should thank you for giving me the push I needed."

"We've decided to keep your secret," Jade says, clearly trying to cheer Madam Lecter up.

And Madam Lecter does brighten, but only a little. "I appreciate that, kids. Thank you."

Before Madam Lecter can plunge too far back into her river of wretchedness, I strike. "Can you give us another lesson on how to find a thinning in the veil?"

"We'll be careful," Leroy adds quickly. "And we won't go anywhere near our families. We've decided we aren't ready for that."

"I wish I was as smart as you three when I first left

the Spirit Institute. It would have saved me a lot of grief." Her gaze jumps from one of us to the next. When it's my turn under her laser eyes, I feel like a piece of moldy bread being studied under a microscope. Finally, Madam Lecter nods. "I think I can trust you to be responsible. Meet me in the mirror room after dinner tonight. Be careful to avoid being followed."

As much as I want to cheer or whoop or twirl in circles like Madison does when she's excited, the vacant expression settling back onto Madam Lecter's face prevents it. I silently return to my desk.

Clearly I'm not the only one suppressing emotions, though, because as soon as we step foot into Room B8 and our eyes have acclimated to being back in the Land of the Living, Jade lets out a squeal. Mister Zilla shoots her a death glare.

"Sorry, Mister Zilla," Jade calls across the room before she turns back to me and Leroy. "I cannot wait for tonight!"

"Me either," Leroy whispers. "I can't believe Madam Lecter agreed so readily."

Mister Zilla must have Superman hearing, because he doubles down on his angry face.

"I believe it." My indoor voice has never been all that indoor, but I try my best. "She—"

Mister Zilla has reached the end of his very short rope. "You three had better stop your blabbering! If you don't start concentrating soon, none of you are passing this class."

Leroy looks horrified, but Jade pats him reassuringly on the back. "Don't worry, Leroy, we aren't failing anything. What Mister Grumpy Pants over there doesn't know is that after tonight, we'll be able to practice in the *real* Land of the Living any time we want."

Leroy's horrified expression melts away.

"Just think of all the adventures we're going to have." Jade begins bouncing up and down like she's swallowed a jackrabbit, and frankly, I'm tempted to bounce with her.

Because as much as I wish I were still alive, since getting pummeled by that coconut, I've made two incredible new friends, we've solved the Mystery of the Disappearing Painting, and we've essentially earned ourselves passports to *the entire world*.

"You're right, Jade. It is going to be amazing!" My excitement gets the better of me, and even though I know it will earn me a reprimand from Mister Zilla, I bang my hand down on the table, exactly like my grandma does whenever she annihilates an opponent in dominos.

At the sound of the squidgy *whack*, five heads swivel in

my direction. Every single one of them wearing a look of shock or delight or jealousy.

"Good job, young sir," Mister Zilla says, and my eyebrows shoot up. Did I hear him correctly? Did *Mister Zilla* just give *me* a compliment? "Maybe there's hope for you yet."

And that's when I realize what I'd done to make Rebecca clench her fists and flare her nostrils.

To make Kevin clap and cheer.

To make Jade bounce up and down like she's swallowed not one jackrabbit, but an entire family of them.

I'd slammed my hand down on the table, and *it didn't go straight through*!

Oh yeah. Me and my friends are definitely having loads of adventures.

Lists of Thanks

Near the end of *Phantom Academy,* Finn creates lists about all the people he loves most in the world. Or rather, a list about all the *still living* people he loves most in the world. It therefore only seemed natural that when I sat down to write this acknowledgment section—the place where I could officially thank just a handful of the MANY, MANY, MANY people who've played a role in making *Phantom Academy* a reality—I'd take a page out of Finn's book... and make a few lists of my own.

The geniuses of the publishing world who've helped me SO MUCH

- Jim McCarthy—agent extraordinaire. Thank you for being endlessly kind, supportive, encouraging, and honest. I don't know what I'd do without you!
- Kara Sargent—aka dream editor. Thank you so much for championing this book and for making it So Much Better with your amazingly thoughtful editorial feedback!
- Jay Kim (cover illustrator) and Tiara Iandiorio (cover designer). Thank you for giving me the most utterly perfect cover EVER!

LISTS OF THANKS

- To the rest of the amazing team at Aladdin and Simon Kids, especially Alex Kelleher, Mike Rosamilia, Art Morgan, Anna Jarzab, Valerie Garfield, and my copyeditor and proofreader: Kimberly Capriola and Penina Lopez. Thank you for all the little things and big things that you do behind the scenes to make author dreams come true!

My fabulous critique partners and writerly friends
- The Noodle Friends, to whom this book has been dedicated. I've said it before, and I'll say it again: I don't think I'd still be writing today if it weren't for you. I'll be eternally grateful for the day we met!
- The Fictionistas. Whether we're strolling through cemeteries or chatting over coffee or shooting emails back and forth, thank you for being the critique group that dreams are made of.
- Liz. I cherish our Tuesday morning writing/gabbing sessions sooo much. Thank you for being such an incredible friend!
- The Lakeside Writing Crew. I can't imagine a better way to start each week than by spending a couple hours with you folks. Thank you for all the laughter, comradery, and coffee.

LISTS OF THANKS

- The Middle Grade Magic Discord group. Thank you for being such a supportive group of PHENOMENAL writers!
- The Rhyme and Punishment critique group. Thank you for taking a newbie picture book writer under your wings and showing me the ropes! It's amazing how much your PB smarts have helped my MG writing.

My incredible family

- My husband. Thank you for being my rock. My Superman. My cheerleader. My heart.
- My children. From liking my dorky Instagram posts to giving me bookmark design suggestions, thank you for all the little and big ways you cheer me on. To the moon, girls.
- My parents, my sister, my brother. Thank you for your unwavering love and support! We make a pretty kick-butt family, if I say so myself.

ENTER TERRIFYING WORLDS AND
EXPLORE THE HORRORS OF
HUMANS AND MONSTERS ALIKE IN THE
**MONSTROUS CLASSICS
COLLECTION.**

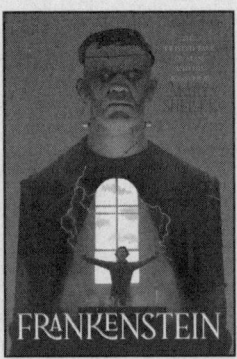

EBOOK EDITIONS AVAILABLE
ALADDIN • SIMONANDSCHUSTER.COM/KIDS